A DREAM COME TRUE

A DREAM COME TRUE

Margaret Carr

CHIVERS

British Library Cataloguing in Publication Data available

This Large Print edition published by BBC Audiobooks Ltd, Bath, 2009.
Published by arrangement with the Author.

U.K. Hardcover ISBN 978 1 408 44142 8
U.K. Softcover ISBN 978 1 408 44143 5

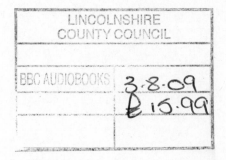

Printed and bound in Great Britain by
CPI Antony Rowe, Chippenham and Eastbourne

For my agent, Juliet Burton

CHAPTER ONE

Cassie Rennington climbed down from the bus and gazed around her. The same names ran across the same shop fronts. The seat still stood under the beech tree in the centre of the green as a new generation of ducks waddled back to the river on the far side of the village. The bus pulled away and Cassie set off for the junction at the bottom of the street. Here set back from the road stood St Peter's church and next to it the vicarage.

Long since deserted by parishioners, the church stood on a slight rise and was surrounded by an iron fence at the front while a high wall enclosed what had once been a graveyard but was now a wilderness of overgrown shrubs and trees. The inscriptions had been recorded and the headstones removed. A for sale sign had been uprooted and lay against the fence.

A wide drive through stone pillars led around the church and across overgrown lawns to a large square house. A green band across the for sale sign read, *sold* and Cassie held her breath as she arrived at the heavy front door and withdrew a key from her pocket. She was home.

Thirty-six years ago she had been born in this house, twelve years later they had left it after her father had died of a heart attack while at his pulpit. She had always dreamt of returning but for many years that was all it had been, a dream. Now she was back and nothing would ever take her away again.

She turned the key in the lock, the door groaned as it slid slowly inward and Cassie stepped into the hall. There were coloured glass panels on either side of the door and these cast shadowed patterns across the tiled floor. The mahogany staircase rose in bare splendour before her.

Of the two rooms one on either side of the hall one was the lounge the other the dining-room while at the back of the house beyond the stairs lay the library and the large room that had been kitchen and living-room to herself, her mother and the four boys.

Her father had spent most of his short life in the church or the library as she remembered. Her mother lived long enough to see her children through college and the oldest boy married with her first grandson on the way, before giving up and dying of cancer.

Cassie let her bags drop to the floor. Memories were cascading through her mind as she ran fingers around the smooth dome of the newel post. Walking through into the library she was shocked at the sight of the shelf lined walls stripped bare of their books. Had it always been such a dark room, she wondered and with a sigh turned to leave.

There was a small conservatory between the library and the kitchen which, with broken glass panes and old pots with shrunken contents, was looking very sad and derelict. The long kitchen with its fire range at one end and a dart board still on the wall at the other hit Cassie so hard that tears trickled silently down her cheeks to fall unnoticed from her jaw.

While staring across the ceramic sink and out of the window to the long garden and orchard at the bottom, she was disturbed by the sound of grinding engine gears on the other side of the wall. What on earth was happening in the graveyard, she wondered. As she made to turn away there was a sickening tearing sound, the engine died, and as she watched, a large conifer began to tilt in her direction.

Agape in horror she saw it crash through the six foot wall, bounce once and come to a quivering halt against a pear tree. She ran for the back door, realised she didn't have a key to unlock it and ran back into the hall to retrieve the envelope from the estate agent. Once back at the rear door she scrabbled in the envelope until she found a key that fit, then flung open the door and headed out into the garden.

A tall man with dark hair was standing at the base of the tree rubbing the back of his neck.

'What on earth do you think you are doing?'

Cassie shouted through the gap in the wall.

'Sorry about this, I was trying to clear . . .'

'Have you got a licence for that thing?' Cassie cried, staring in disbelief at the yellow giant of a machine on the other side of the wall.

'Look, instead of screaming at me through this gap why don't you come around and we can discuss what we are going to do about it.'

'We . . .' Cassie was lost for words. After scowling furiously at him she flung out her arms and stamped back into the house. Marching through the house she kicked her bags to one side, left the front door open and heading down a narrow cinder path came to a small wicket gate. The path continued up to the vestry door, which of course was locked. Continuing along the wall of the church she came to the wilderness at the back.

A large double gate at the rear of the property was open onto a narrow lane. Just inside the gate stood a beautiful cream and brown caravan. On the doorstep of this vehicle sat the man, responsible for the demolishing of her wall, tugging boots from his feet. A lot of shrubbery had already been cleared by the yellow monster sitting across her path.

He had the cheek to wave to her as she ploughed her way through loose branches and rutted soil.

'Can I offer you something to drink?' He stood up as she came to rest in front of him.

4

'No thank you,' she snapped. 'What I want to know is what you are going to do about my wall.'

He turned back into the caravan. 'Tea, coffee or beer?'

She felt silly talking to an empty doorway so climbed up into the van. 'I've told you, nothing thank you. Will you see to the removal of that tree and the rebuilding of my wall or do you want me to get estimates from local builders to do the job?'

Shrugging his shoulders he helped himself to a beer, pulled the tab and walked off to the sitting area of the van.

Furious, she followed him.

'For heaven's sake, sit down. If we are going to be neighbours then we had better learn to get along. I'll saw up the tree and remove it myself then I'll try and find someone to help me build up your wall.'

Plonking herself down on a seat she said, 'It will have to be a proper job, I don't want some amateur effort that will fall down six months later.'

'It will be a professional job, I promise you.'

'Are you the contractor?'

'I'm the owner, I've just bought the property and I'm hoping to . . .'

'Then what on earth are you thinking about hiring a machine like that when you're obviously not qualified to drive it.' Cassie noticed a nerve jerking along his jaw and

5

decided that enough was enough and a hasty retreat might be the better part of valour. She stood up to leave.

'I'm planning on renovating the church. There'll be a lot of noise and mess for a while I'm afraid, I hope it won't be too inconvenient for you,' he said, totally ignoring her earlier comment. He stood up as he said this and placed his beer can on a nearby table.

'You're going to live in the church?'

'I am.'

*   *   *

Once outside she turned to face him. 'Will you be extending out here?'

'No, this will be the garden.'

'You won't feel uncomfortable sunbathing over . . .'

'In a graveyard,' he gave her a quizzical look. 'No, what could be more suitable for a garden.'

'Quite,' she said, feeling the uncomfortable one now.

Back in the house she carried her bags upstairs then wandered from room to room deciding which one she would have for herself. The large front bedroom that had belonged to her parents and whose windows looked down the front drive was attractive but ghosts held her back. The second front room had a window looking over to the church and this she didn't like.

Finally the one she chose was a back bedroom that had two windows—one looking down the back garden and a side window that looked over the wall to the fields and hills beyond, and in the distance the river where they had paddled when they were children. This had been her room all those years ago and would be hers again she promised herself.

The van with her belongings, the only ones she had wanted to keep, would be arriving at two o'clock. It felt strange to think of that man tearing out the heart of the church to make a home in it. How would he do it, she wondered. Would the alterations be all internal and if so would he need permission. She could check at the council offices to see if they had any plans. Surely as a concerned neighbour she had a right to ask.

She wiped her fingers along the windowsill, the place needed a good clean. She went back downstairs with a notebook and pen. In the lounge she sat in the window seat and began to scribble down a list of all there was to do and organise in the following weeks. From her seat she would see the van when it came.

The van duly arrived and disgorged a bed, table, two chairs, a rocking chair, a chest and several boxes. The bed, chest and two of the boxes were taken up to the bedroom, the rest deposited in the kitchen. Rummaging in one of the boxes she unearthed pans, a kettle, cooking utensils and some food. She used the packing to try out the range and to her surprise it took hold straight away. Quickly she fed it some more then with a firm mouth marched outside and up to the fallen tree.

The man was back at work sawing away at the top of the tree.

'I would like some of that for my fire.'

He looked up from his task.

'I don't think you need it, look,' and he pointed over her shoulder.

Cassie let out a squeak of fear as she watched the flames shooting from the chimney pot.

The man had dropped his saw and was running over to the kitchen. Cassie chased after him. Turning on the kitchen tap he thrust pans beneath the water then swung them over to the fire where he threw the contents on to the range. This doused the fire in the grate but as he explained, the chimney itself was still on fire.

'Didn't you think to get it swept first, goodness knows how many years' soot has accumulated up there.'

'What do I do now, will it go out by itself?'

'Other than call the fire service, how the devil do I know, an old house like this could have wood beams criss crossing the chimney, if they catch hold the whole place could go up.' He flung the pan back into the sink.

They moved out into the garden and looked

upward. 'Well the pot's not red, that's a good sign, if you ask me you've been very lucky. It should die down itself.'

'Thank you for your help,' she mumbled and slunk away into the kitchen. Inside she leant back against the closed door and breathed a sigh of relief.

Later she kicked herself for not bringing her old electric fire for after the sun went down it grew quite cold. All the utilities had been turned on before her arrival but of course the vicarage had never had central heating. Now she lay shivering beneath her duvet, the ticking of her alarm clock on the chest echoing in the otherwise empty room.

The following morning it rained. Cassie set to with a vengeance refusing to be disheartened. Sweeping and scrubbing, the immersion heater had given plenty of hot water and she had brought the cleaning tools with her. She was cleaning windows when a little dirty white van rolled up to the front door. A small man jumped out and rang the bell.

Frowning, Cassie ceased what she was doing and went to answer the door.

'Alf Manners, Mrs, come to do the chimneys.'

He turned back to his van but halted when Cassie called, 'I'm sorry, Mr Manners did you say, but I didn't book you.'

'Oh, I know that Mrs, it was the bloke next

door, said if I didn't come you'd as like as not set fire to the whole damn place.'

'Well I like that,' Cassie steamed.

The little man was watching her expectantly. 'Do you want them done or not, Mrs, I've got plenty more jobs to be doing.'

She sighed and signalled him inside.

'There's some stock of work here, Mrs,' he said after touring the house and arriving back in the kitchen.

Cassie nodded. 'Do your worst, Mr Manners, we might as well start off with a clean sweep.'

'There won't be any mess mind but it'll cost you a fair bit.'

'That's all right. The, er, man next door, how did he know about you?'

Alf Manners grinned. 'I'm a fan of him, I've been helping him out, bits of jobs and that.'

'A fan?' Cassie asked, bewildered.

'Aye, I go to all his concerts, well the ones round about anyway.'

'Concerts?'

The little man stood back away. 'Don't tell me you didn't recognise him.'

'Should I?'

'Marc Dominic, the Domino they always call him because he wears black and white at performances. Why, he was on telly two weeks ago being interviewed on that tea time show.'

'He's a pop star?' Cassie whispered.

'He's a guitarist, writes his own music, lovely

10

stuff, you must have heard of him.'

Cassie was shaking her head slowly, trying to digest all this new information about her neighbour.

CHAPTER TWO

With her basic cleaning finished Cassie's next job was to find a plumber. This was harder than she had anticipated. So on seeing Alf Manners' van outside the church one morning she decided to go over and make enquiries of him.

The main door stood open so she stepped inside and called his name. There was a lot of banging and sawing going on and in the end she had to shout hard to make herself heard. A voice called from upstairs and as she waited for someone to appear she glanced around at the barely recognisable church.

All the furnishings had been stripped out, skirting and floor boards were up in many places and the whole looked as if it had been attacked by vandals.

'Would you like a look around?'

His voice startled her. 'I was looking for Alf.'

'You wouldn't be trying to steal my helper would you?'

'No, I only want to ask his advice. I need a

plumber.'

He leant back against the wall, hands in pockets, and nodded his head. 'Well you've found one, Alf does all the plumbing around here, unfortunately he has his hands full at the moment.'

'Alf is a plumber?'

'That's right.'

She stiffened up, angered at the half smile flitting across the man's mouth.

'Well perhaps he can tell me of someone else who could help me.'

Glancing down at the tips of his workman's boots he said, 'It will be a lot more expensive getting someone from town.'

'No problem, can I speak with Alf?'

'Alf,' he called back up the stairs. 'The lady wants a word.'

There was the thump of dropped tools then Alf appeared at the top of the stairs. 'What can I do for you, Mrs?'

'The lady wants the name of a plumber.'

Angry at his interference Cassie called up, 'Mr Domino says you are too busy to help me . . .'

A howl of laughter came hurtling down the stairs and Cassie scowled at the man who had turned his back to her.

'What's so funny?' she demanded.

'The name's Marc Dominic,' he replied.

'That's what I said.'

'You called me Mr Domino.'

'Oh well, whatever.'

'I'll be over lunch time, see what you need, Mrs,' called Alf, the laughter still in his voice.

She nearly told him not to bother, the rude little man, then she thought better of it and made to leave.

'Sure you wouldn't like to see round the place?'

'No thank you.'

Alf arrived in his van then sat chewing a sandwich and drinking from a flask before clearing them away and pulling out a newspaper. He read that for all of ten minutes then folded it and placed it on the seat next to him among numerous other bits and pieces.

Cassie watched from her position in the window seat. When at last he climbed from the van she left what she was doing and went to meet him.

'Which fires will you be blocking up, Mrs?'

'None of them. I want the central heating as back up only.'

'Expensive back up, the piping is in fairly good nick for such an old house, radiators in every room then?'

'Towel rail in the bathroom.'

'What about the kitchen, do you want anything in there, don't usually bother in kitchens, but it is a big room.'

'Two at the far end away from the range.'

'You keeping that thing?'

'The house will stay just as it has always

13

been with as few alterations as possible.'

The little man's head nodded as he scribbled away in his note book. Then he looked up grinning. 'Mr Dominic would approve of that.'

Cassie bristled. 'Mr Dominic's approval or otherwise is of no concern to me Alf.'

'Of course not, Mrs, just he's trying to do the same sort of thing next door.'

'How long is all this going to take and when can you start?'

'Well let me see,' he lifted up his cap and scratched in his hair before replacing the cap with a tug. 'If I get the lads along to do the rough while I finish helping Mr D, then I can get the essential work done by, what day is it today, with a bit of luck four weeks, if I work out the materials tonight and order them tomorrow.'

'How much upheaval will all this necessitate?'

He glanced around. 'You got furniture coming. Well I wouldn't go laying any carpets but not too much mess, Mrs.'

The following morning she caught the bus into town. Her first stop was the Post Office, there was a large black telephone sat in the hall at the Vicarage but no books. She had rung BT and been told the books would be delivered within the next two days. The phone box in the village had been vandalised so at the Post Office she looked up the numbers she needed. Next came a visit to the local garage and a guide through second hand cars. A small yellow Citroën appealed and after arranging to have it inspected by an AA mechanic, she left.

A call at the council offices revealed no outward changes to the church apart from a swimming pool in what used to be the old church hall. The yard that had separated the church from the hall was to be covered, thus creating more living space.

'That's a lot of space for just one man,' she commented to the girl showing her the plans.

The girl giggled. 'One man, he has five children, everyone knows that.'

Cassie groaned inwardly, not another fan.

'Then of course he will need a soundproof area for his music.'

'How on earth does his poor wife put up with it all.'

'Oh he doesn't have a wife.'

'He's a widower?'

'No, he's single,' she said with a sigh.

Cassie decided not to think about that piece of information and with a quick goodbye left the building. On the bus going home however she couldn't stop her mind wandering back to her irresponsible neighbour. How could a man have five children and no wife, very easily these days she supposed. The life these pop stars led anything was possible.

Once home Cassie put a call through to the AA and arranged to have someone call at the garage and inspect the car she had chosen, then she rang a local driving school and booked several lessons.

Four calls to interior decorators resulted in waiting lists of many months ahead. Well she could do nothing about that for the present, she decided. Next on her agenda was the garden.

There used to be a nursery garden on the outskirts of the village at one time and she wondered if it still existed. While shopping in the high street she asked about the nursery and discovered there was now a housing estate where the gardens had once been.

Feeling down at this news she noticed across the village green a general store with brooms, baskets and boxes outside on the pavement. Henderson's had always been a store of great excitement to children years ago, when like Aladdin's Cave it sold everything from fire screens to bicycles and crockery to toy soldiers.

Bending down over the boxes she now saw contained autumn flowering plants she failed to notice the approach of her neighbour.

'I'm going over to Benton Gardens later if you would like a lift.'

Startled, Cassie shot upright, he was standing right behind her, tall and dark with the most amazing green eyes she had ever seen.

'I've finished sawing the tree and have ordered some more stone to replace the broken pieces. That's what I'm going over to collect. They have a good stock of plants, are you looking for anything in particular?'

Yes, Cassie thought, you could see how women would flock to him. He was a real charmer.

'No, thank you.' Then as he turned away she called, 'I don't suppose Alf does decorating as well.'

He looked over his shoulder. 'He does most things, for nearly anyone,' he said before walking off.

Cassie stuck her tongue out at his retreating back before hurriedly glancing around to make sure no-one had seen her. She hadn't seen any children, it was probably all hype by agents and media to puff up his sexy image. Disgusted with her thoughts she wiped them from her mind.

The delivery of the Citroën was a great delight to Cassie who decided to name her Daffodil because of her colour. Climbing inside she familiarised herself with all the knobs and pedals and was confident that it would take only a few lessons and she would be free to travel where she would.

The dirty white van drew up behind the Citroën the following day and Alf and a tall gangly youth climbed out. They walked around the car inspecting it here and there before giving it their approval. Cassie came to meet them from the corner of the house where she had been trimming some ivy.

'Nice little number that,' Alf offered. 'Get it local did you?'

'Yes, at the garage in town.'

'Had it looked over, I hope.'

'Yes thank you, by the AA.'

'Ah yes, that's good. Would cost you for them, should have let me know, I'd have done it for you.'

Cassie didn't know whether to laugh or cry, was there anything this little man didn't do. She knew exactly what was coming next and held her breath.

'Mr D said you needed some decorating done.'

She closed her eyes for a second to control herself. 'That's right.'

'Well old Mrs Thwaites has a leaky sink and I promised to help Bill Fenwick with his roof, but we could measure up today and Jack here will bring you round some pattern books tonight, that right lad?'

'Aye, Uncle Alf.'

They started the plumbing earlier than expected and Cassie had dragged the rocking chair out into the late autumn sunshine. Wallpaper pattern books and paint cards lay all around her as she closed her eyes and visualised what the house would look like when it was finished. It had been a frustrating few weeks managing with bare floorboards and only essential necessities around her, but soon

18

she would be able to relax and enjoy her dream.

CHAPTER THREE

It was with a prickly sensation that she knew she was no longer alone and her eyes flew open. A small inquisitive face filled her vision.

'I thought you were dead.' And the lower lip quivered.

Cassie sat upright. 'No, I'm not dead,' she spoke gently, 'who are you?'

'My name's Ruthie. My mammy is dead.'

'Well I'm very sorry to hear that. Who looks after you now?'

'Mae Choo. Do you live here?'

'Yes, I do,' Cassie said with a smile.

'Do you have any children?'

'No I'm afraid I don't.'

'I can come and live with you if you're lonely.'

Before Cassie could form a reply a slim Eurasian girl came through the gate from the church. 'Please I apologise for your disturbance. Mr Dominic will be blocking in the gateway soon. Ruthie come along.'

This was said without the glimmer of a smile and Cassie was made to feel as though she had already complained at the child's presence. 'She didn't disturb me really. Do you

19

work for Mr Dominic?'

This question received only a smile and a nod of the head as Mae took hold of Ruthie's hand and led her away. Cassie watched them cross to the gate and disappear down the side of the church. Well that didn't bode well for good relations, she thought. Perhaps it was just as well the man intended to block up the gate. But she couldn't help sighing at the thought of not talking to Ruthie again.

The fireplaces gleamed, their grates set and ready to light at a moment's notice. Radiators were all in place and a hot towel rail offered warmth from alongside a claw foot bath. Two of Alf's nephews were stripping wallpaper and preparing wood. The mosaic tiles in the hall had been scoured and sealed by Cassie and now glowed with warm colour.

She sat in the window seat in the lounge and stared out over the rain soaked garden, a list of jobs lay in her lap, most of the work had been crossed out, and she wondered what she would do when it was finished. Her dream had been of owning the house and taking it back to its former glory. Learning to drive a car would give her independence, and a pet for company. She hadn't looked much beyond that.

The rain stopped and she decided to walk down to the village. Henderson's, the doctor's surgery and the paper shop lay on the far side of the green, while on the main road through the village lay a small supermarket, butchers, bakers/café and a boutique. The village also boasted four guest houses and two public houses. The pubs were the 'Rose and Crown', and the 'Green Man'.

The 'Rose and Crown' had a three star restaurant, held a reading group once a month, the camera club every two weeks and a Rotary meeting every other Tuesday. The 'Green Man' on the other hand had a darts team, held bingo on a Wednesday night and a quiz on Fridays. All this information had been passed to Cassie while in the baker's buying buns for her workers.

So she was slightly surprised to see Marc Dominic coming out of the 'Green Man' as she left the shop, she would have thought the 'Rose and Crown' more fitting for a pop star. When he crossed the road to come alongside her she was slightly taken aback.

'I believe you had a visit from Ruthie a while back. She's a very inquisitive child. She never stops talking about the lady who lives by herself.'

'She's a lovely girl. Your helper inferred you would be blocking up the gateway. I'd rather you didn't, I can easily put a lock on it if you are worried about the children's security.'

He laughed. 'It was for your privacy as much as anything.' His face straightened again and a small frown drew down his brows. 'Mae, while a great help to me, is my daughter, not a paid helper.'

21

Cassie tripped on the kerb and his hand came out automatically to steady her. She gave him a half smile as she found her footing.

'I see you have a car now.'

'Yes, I'm learning to drive. My instructor says I should be ready to take my test shortly.'

'You should get out and practice, it's quiet enough around here and it helps you gain confidence.'

'You can't drive by yourself,' she said, as they made their way back to the vicarage. 'You have to have a driver in with you.'

'Well I'm sure . . .'

'Oh please, not Alf again.'

He gave a pleasant chuckle. 'What I was about to say was I could spare you the odd half hour if you'd like.'

Cassie was struck dumb by his offer and could only mutter a quick 'thank you' before leaving him at the front of the church and hurrying round to the entrance of the vicarage. What have I done, she asked herself as she hung her coat over the newel post.

'Tea, Mrs,' the oldest of Alf's nephews called from the kitchen. Raising her eyes heavenward Cassie picked up the bag of buns and headed down the hall.

'What about the back room, Mrs?' Our Jack, the youngest of Alf's nephews, meant the library. 'Do you want them shelves left or are they to come down?'

The other nephew nudged him. 'It's on the

22

plan, they're staying, isn't that right, Mrs?'

Cassie was doling out buns and decided that the 'Mrs' was a gene thing, she might even get to miss it after they were finished.

The fallen tree in the back garden was all sawn up and her neighbour had halved the logs between them. Now, she noticed as she washed through the cups in the sink, the gap in the wall was finished also and everything was back as it should be.

The telephone rang at half-past two the following afternoon. Cassie had forgotten all about the offered drive so was taken aback when Marc Dominic spoke.

'If you've recovered from lunch I have a spare half hour if you still want to go out.'

On the point of thinking up some lame excuse she found herself agreeing to join him. She replaced the phone, while calling herself all the names she could think of and grabbing a jacket flung it on. Taking the keys from their hook by the kitchen door she saw her hands were shaking. This wouldn't do, she would have to get a grip, still talking herself down she went out to the car.

He was standing by the bonnet of the Citroën. His hair hung over the collar of the roll necked sweater and work weary jeans clad his long legs. 'I didn't dress for the occasion,' he said with a twist to the corner of his mouth.

She unlocked the car and they climbed in. Momentary panic cleared everything from her head. They sat silent and still, nothing happened. Then Marc slid round in his seat, back against the door and looked across at her. 'Take it easy, it'll pass.'

Taking a deep breath Cassie stuck out her chin and pushed the key into the ignition. The drive went well and Cassie was smiling as she turned back in through the vicarage gates.

'Alf tells me the work on your house is progressing well and that you have kept as much to the old style of the place as possible. This is what I'm trying to do next door. As a church I want to keep all the stained glass and beautiful carving and stone work while making it safe and comfortable for the children who have a variety of needs and of course my own. I would still like to show you around sometime and hear your thoughts on what we are doing.'

She felt pressurised into inviting him to look around her own home and for some reason did not want that he should. 'Thank you. I'd like that, but for now I must get back to the workmen and see what they are up to.'

'Yes of course,' she thought he sounded disappointed, 'we'll do this again.' He climbed out of the car and headed across to the gate in the wall.

Cassie watched him go then called after him, 'Thank you for your time.'

He lifted a casual hand in acknowledgement and kept walking.

Cassie locked the car and turned into the

24

house.

The decorating was finished, the floor coverings had arrived, rugs downstairs on newly polished floors and fitted carpets in the bedrooms. Now she only awaited the arrival of her furniture. On Thursday morning she woke to the rattle of rain on her window. By the look of the flooding around the back door and the bog of a garden at the front it had been throwing it down all night. This didn't bode well for the delivery van and the safe handling of her furniture. Laying plastic and dust sheets over exposed flooring and carpets she crossed her fingers there wouldn't be too much of a mess.

The morning passed quickly and she ate lunch in the kitchen. By two o'clock she was beginning to wonder where they were. By four she was angry and on the phone to the removal people. She was kept waiting while they checked up for her, then to her astonishment she was told the furniture had been delivered.

An argument ensued that ended with Cassie slamming down the receiver. Her furniture had been delivered next door. Of all the stupid, Cassie fumed, then stopped short as a new thought struck her. What were they thinking of next door to allow such a thing to happen. Someone must have let the removal men in, didn't they realise it wasn't their stuff. Where on earth was the silly man when this was happening.

Donning coat and hat she pulled on her boots and headed out into the still pouring rain. It was getting late now and the heavy sky drew on an early evening, as Cassie squelched across the grass towards the wicket gate. The gate was locked with a bright new chain and lock that would have kept the prisoners of Dartmoor secure.

Groaning under her breath she turned down the drive, on to the road then around to the church. By now the rain was running off her coat hem and soaking the trousers around her knees.

She climbed the steps to the church door where she looked for something to pull or push. Nothing, typical of the man. Now what? There was no shelter and she was more uncomfortable by the minute. On impulse she reached out and twisted the large iron ring of a handle. The sneck lifted and the door swung quietly open.

Peering inside she first coughed then knocked. There was no reply, the place was as silent as the grave. Venturing further inside she called out. Still no reply. She was in a vestibule screened off from the body of the church by beautiful panelling and stained glass.

Opening the double doors she was faced by a magnificent staircase leading up the centre of the room where once she had knelt and prayed. There were rooms to the right and left of this staircase and behind it the door that had once led to the Sunday School. Unable to stop herself Cassie moved towards this door.

The door led into a large kitchen cum family room with a conservatory where once the organ pipes had stood. The conservatory was large and housed all kinds of comfortable seating, tables covered in jig-saws, colouring books and magazines. There were boxes of toys and shelves of books. Well, Cassie thought, the children didn't seem to want for anything, except perhaps a mother.

A slight noise had her swing round. In the doorway to the kitchen stood the girl Mae. 'Can I help you?' There was neither disapproval nor friendliness in her tone.

'I'm sorry, I shouldn't be here, but there was no answer to my knock and I did call out.' She felt decidedly uncomfortable under the girl's calm stare. 'The thing is the removal people delivered my furniture here instead of next door. Is, um, your father here?'

Stupid question, she berated herself, if he was he would be facing her and not this child.

'Marc will be down directly. Your furniture is stored in one of the front rooms.' With that she turned and left Cassie standing stunned in the entrance to the conservatory.

Gathering herself together she moved on into the kitchen cum family room and sat down in the nearest chair. And this was where Marc found her. 'Well this is nice, you've come

27

to have a look round the place, good.'

The anger at the loss of her misplaced furniture had receded as she gazed around what had been achieved in the old church. Now it reared its head again as she realised he had been home after all.

'Why on earth didn't you redirect my furniture instead of letting them leave it here?'

'Ah, so you didn't come to see my home.' He filled a nearby kettle and plugged it in. 'Can I offer you something to drink?'

'No thank you.'

'I wasn't in when your stuff arrived. I was collecting the children from school. Mae thought the delivery was mine, I should have come around earlier to tell you it was here.'

'The thing is, what am I supposed to do about it now? I have just had a blazing row with the removal people who won't accept responsibility and have point blank refused to come back. The things are too heavy to carry across and it's still pouring with rain.' As she flung this last sentence to him Cassie was near to tears.

He placed a cup of tea in front of her before returning with milk and sugar.

'Best antidote for a bad day I find.' He sat down opposite. 'Don't worry about the stuff, I'll have it sent over first thing in the morning.'

She sniffed and blew her nose, flinging back the forelock of wet hair as she did so. A round dark face with curly black hair and big brown

28

eyes peeped around the door. Then the soft voice of Mae called from the hall and the face disappeared.

Cassie stared at the man across the table hardly daring to believe what she was thinking. That amused twist was back on his lips as he looked up from his tea.

'I have to get back,' she stammered.

He rose with her. 'But you haven't seen the pool area or the upstairs yet.'

'That's very kind of you but perhaps another time.'

He saw her to the door and watched as she fled down the path.

The furniture arrived as promised the following morning in a large yellow hire van. The two men who accompanied it seemed well versed in furniture removal, much to Cassie's relief for many of the pieces were valuable antiques. They had been bought, and some restored at various times in the last eighteen months and all had been put into storage until the house was ready.

As each piece was placed where she had visualised it the dream came nearer to reality. The rain had stopped and the ground was drying nicely, making the men's work that much easier. When they were finished and had driven away in their van, Cassie rolled up the dust sheets and moved around the house admiring each room in turn.

She placed stationery in the drawer of the

29

small walnut writing table in the lounge. A normally sunny room, she had picked out a pale Wedgwood blue décor, while in the dining room the rich mahogany dining suite glowed against pastel green. China from a box in the kitchen was placed in a cabinet and a beautiful crystal candelabrum occupied the centre of the table.

In the hall she had picked out a paler shade from one of the tiles for the walls, with a deeper shade for the stair carpet. She had toyed with the idea of replacing some of the wallpaper but turned it down in favour of paint. The house looked so much lighter she knew she had made the right decision.

The kitchen was furnished now with a large wooden table, six wheel backed chairs, an extremely large kitchen press and an American fridge freezer to complement the pantry. The small conservatory had been turned into a downstairs cloakroom, while in the library Cassie's books looked lost scattered across the many shelves. It was time for her evening meal.

She returned to the kitchen and as she sat down at the table and helped herself to the chicken salad she had prepared earlier the excitement of her success faded. Once again she asked herself, 'What now?'

CHAPTER FOUR

The twins from next door had red hair and freckles and were chasing something across her garden when Cassie first met them. She was attempting to cut the hedge on the far side of her property when the pair dashed past in hot pursuit of a flash of green.

'What is it?' she called. 'What are you after?'

The green streak tried to shoot up a tree only to fall to the ground again. It twisted mid air and ran straight for Cassie. That's when she saw what it was and lunged forward catching it against her chest. Quickly she pulled up her sweater to enfold the terrified cat.

'What on earth's happened?' she asked the panting twins as they came alongside her.

'It got in the way when we were painting,' said the boy.

'It made a mess in the van,' said the girl.

'We were going to wash it,' they both chipped in.

They were all walking back to the house. Cassie hesitated, not wanting them all trouping through her beautiful hall. So she steered them around to the back and into the kitchen. Here she stood the cat in the sink and for the first time took a measure of the damage.

The poor thing was covered from head to tail in slimy green gloss paint. What in heavens name was she to do? The cat meowed pitifully. Cassie set the children to do her bidding as they gathered scissors, cloths and turpentine. Then she set to work clipping and scrubbing the reluctant cat. It was a terrible mess when she had finished and set it down on the floor. It fled straight under the kitchen press and refused to come out.

'How can we take her home if we can't get her out,' demanded the boy.

'Well you will just have to leave her here,' Cassie said.

The girl began to cry so Cassie offered them a biscuit each. 'What are your names?' she asked.

'I'm Donald and she's Dorothy,' the boy replied.

'And how old are you?'

'We're ten, but I'm the oldest.'

'And do you always speak for your sister?'

'Usually,' he agreed, 'she's shy.'

Cassie had to smile at his cheeky boldness. 'Well, I think you had better go home now and own up to the dreadful mess you must have left behind you.'

Donald screwed up his nose and Dorothy looked near to tears again, but they left without a word and once the door shut behind them Cassie was down on her knees at the press trying to find the cat. Later she placed a saucer of milk and a dish of tuna on the floor next to the press and left the cat to recover.

Next morning she came into the kitchen to find a beautiful if somewhat raggy tabby sitting on her windowsill in the sunshine. Cassie wouldn't have believed it possible for last night's wreck to turn out so well.

'We shall have to give you a name if you are going to stay around,' Cassie told the cat. 'What do you think of Marquis? That was the cat in Puss in Boots.'

'More like Danger Cat, if you saw the mess in my van.' Marc's voice boomed through the window. The cat jumped down with a screech and Cassie placed a finger against her lips. 'You're frightening it,' she scolded.

'I'll do more than frighten it, I'll wring its neck,' he said, as she let him in through the back door.

'It couldn't have been the cat's fault. What were your children doing with gloss paint anyway?'

She scowled after the fleeing cat who retreated to the press. 'I had some old paint stacked under the van and the twins found it. They have been punished and won't do it again.'

'Sounds like you were negligent leaving it there in the first place,' she scolded.

He was smiling at her and she gave her loose hair an angry tug into place. 'I called to see if you had incurred any damage dealing with all that paint. It couldn't have been easy cleaning up after them.'

'No harm done,' she said, glancing suggestively at the door.

But he wasn't taking the hint. 'I thought you might show me around the changes Alf and family have made. He did tell me but I would very much like to see for myself. Then perhaps if you're free, in say an hour, we could go out in the car again.'

Cassie bit her lip. How could she have let herself get into this kind of position? She had invaded his home, there was no getting away from that, and become beholden to him for driving escort, now whether she wanted to or not the least she could do in return was to show him around the house.

He said little as they wandered around from room to room, then after glancing into the library and new cloakroom they were back in the kitchen.

'I was wondering what a single woman like yourself could possibly want such a large house for?' he answered to her enquiry as to what he thought of the house.

'I was born here and always dreamt of coming back one day.'

'You're a vicar's daughter,' he asked, his voice tinged with surprise.

'My father died when I was twelve, that's when we left.'

'Excuse me for asking, but do you work?'

She felt like telling him to mind his own business but said coolly, 'I'm a teacher.'

'Round here?'

'Not at the moment.'

'Well, if you are looking for work I might be able to help, what subjects do you teach?'

Cassie could feel the hysteria mounting, if he didn't go soon she was going to scream. 'English and Geography, but I don't need any work at the moment, thank you.'

At last he took the hint. 'I'll come back at ten and we can take that drive,' he said, before letting himself out of the door.

* * *

'I'm going away tomorrow. When are you due to take your test?' he asked on their return from a satisfactory drive.

'In a fortnight's time, the twenty-second.'

'Well, the best of luck.'

'Who looks after the children while you're away?'

'I have a very reliable workforce and Mae is good with the children.'

'Oh, I see,' Cassie said. 'I haven't seen any signs of a workforce,' she mumbled to herself once he was out of sight. It would be just like the man to think Mae could handle everything for him and she didn't seem old enough to leave to such a heavy responsibility. Perhaps she would pop over there from time to time just to make sure she was coping.

As it happened, when next she went round to the church, now called *Pete's Park*, her ring on the modern push bell was answered by a tall dignified man who asked her her business. Taken aback, Cassie managed to stammer that she was a neighbour and that she had called to check on the children.

'Would that be Miss Cassie?' the man asked.

'Cassie Rennington, yes.'

'Please come in, Miss Rennington. Mr Dominic left strict instructions that you were to be made welcome should you call. The name is James Munro and I have worked for Marc in several capacities for many years. We also have Mrs O'Conner who cooks for us and there is the girl, Viki, she escorts the little ones.'

Cassie could feel embarrassment wrap around her like an ill fitting blanket.

'Ruthie and Sam are out for the afternoon but the twins are upstairs with Mae, shall I call them?'

'No, no, please don't interrupt them. I can see the children are well catered for, Mr Munro.' And as tactfully as possible she made her departure. That will teach you to go poking your nose into things that don't concern you, she scolded herself.

It was October now and she had passed her driving test with ease. There had been no sign of Marc Dominic nor his family apart from the occasional passing in the street and she had not ventured again to *Pete's Park*.

Hard work had put the garden to sleep, quiet but respectable with enough new bulbs to promise an enjoyable spring. The cat, while not the most sociable of creatures nevertheless remained faithful and rarely ventured beyond the confines of the garden.

The house, even with only the one resident, still demanded constant attention and to this end Cassie had hired a woman from the village who was glad of the extra money to come in twice a week and do the rough.

She, in turn, had volunteered her services to tutor children on long stays in the local hospital. This and her new-found fascination with her family history kept most of her time occupied.

Until one day in the middle of the month when she met Mae in the village high street dragging a little dog along on a lead. The dog looked sad and unhappy and Mae looked angry. She turned to watch the girl storm past and wondered where she was going.

When Cassie realised the cat was here to stay she had discovered a veterinary surgery three days a week in a room behind the paper shop. Here she had taken the cat for a check up and his injections.

Now, as she watched Mae cross the green she realised that this was where the girl was going.

She turned into the butcher's to buy some mince for dinner and when she came out Mae was coming back across the green without the dog. Cassie was uncertain as to why she was following the way Mae had gone but some instinct had her entering the vet's door.

The girl at reception recognised her and greeted her warmly.

'Excuse me, I hope you don't think me rude, but a girl was just in with a little dog and I thought I recognised it, is something wrong with it?'

The receptionist's face straightened. 'Oh, no,' she said, 'beautiful little scrap, such a nice nature and all, what a shame.'

'Shame,' Cassie echoed.

'Yes, she explained one of the children had bought it without permission. She brought it in to be put down, but we won't if we can possibly help it, we'll try and find it another home first.'

Cassie was shocked at her neighbour's callousness. 'Poor little thing.'

The receptionist's face brightened. 'I don't suppose . . .' she gave Cassie a pleading look.

Cassie came to with a start. 'Oh no, I couldn't, I have a cat.'

The receptionist was laughing. 'We have six cats and two dogs and three geese. It's not true what they say about cats and dogs you know, they do learn to tolerate each other when they live in the same family. I'm sure your cat would accept the little chap, he's so friendly, wouldn't hurt a fly.'

Cassie didn't see how the receptionist could vouch for that seeing as how she had only just met him herself.

When she produced him from a cage in the back room like a rabbit from a hat, Cassie jumped back startled. When, after a few snuffles and tail wagging, he sat down on the counter and looked at her, she could feel her heart melting.

He went into the vet and was pronounced a fit and healthy eighteen-month-old cross Westie. He was a grey brown colour and his coat was straighter than a true Westie but he had the perky attentiveness of the breed. She decided to call him MacBeth because of his Scottish ancestry, and left with MacBeth and all his furnishings, collar, lead and a large bag of dog food.

Marquis took an instant dislike to MacBeth and flew up the front of the dresser knocking down several cups and saucers on the way. Cassie felt like sitting down and crying. When was she going to learn not to let her impulsiveness rule her life?

Taking a firm hold on herself she did the only thing she could think of and, opening the back door, shooed them both outside.

After she had made herself a cup of tea and calmed down she went out to find them. The cat was sat on top of the wall. It gave her a reproachful look and a complaining meow but wouldn't come down.

MacBeth she discovered barking and yapping excitedly at the side gate. On the other side of the gate Sam sat on his hunkers fondling the little dog through the bars.

'Sam, does anyone know you're here?'

He shook his head. 'I heard him bark and I knew it was him.'

'Are you the one that bought him.'

'Yes, I saved up my pocket money and the man in the shop said he would keep him for me.' He looked up at her then, his large brown eyes filling with unshed tears. 'But Mae stole him from me. Did she bring him to you?'

Cassie hadn't the heart to tell him the truth, so she agreed with him.

'I'm glad you have him. I know you'll look after him and I can come round and see him all the time, can't I?' he asked, suddenly unsure.

'Of course you can, but you must tell your father where you are going first.'

He nodded enthusiastically. 'And can I take him for walks and play in the garden with him?'

Cassie laughed. 'Sometimes.'

Mae approached like a shadow and scolding him gently, led him away.

The next day a large bunch of flowers arrived. Attached to them was a card that read, *Sorry I missed the driving test. Thank you for saving the dog. Marc Dominic.*

Cassie wasn't quite sure how to take this. Did he mean he wanted the dog back, that Mae had taken it without permission? So, armed with the new telephone books she decided to ring him up and ask him. Her call was answered by Mr Munro.

'I'm afraid Marc hasn't returned from his tour yet, Miss Rennington. He isn't due home until the end of the week.'

'Then who sent the flowers, Mr Munro, and how did he know about the dog?'

'The flowers would be Interflora, Miss, and he would know about the dog from the wee lad. He rings the children every night.'

'Of course,' she said, feeling foolish.

After replacing the telephone she picked up the flowers and took them into the kitchen. Did she have a vase, she didn't think so. No-one had ever sent her flowers before. She buried her nose in them and was disappointed that they had very little smell. Still, they looked beautiful and she decided there and then to go out and buy a vase for them.

On Sunday afternoon, coming home from visiting a friend in the next village, she was surprised to find Mae on her doorstep.

'Hello, what can I do for you?' she asked as she climbed out of the car.

'I have told Marc I do not want the children coming into your garden now you have the dog in case they get bitten.' She spoke softly but that did not hide the sting in her words. 'It is a

41

pity you did not think to ask me before you took the animal into your home. It had already bitten Ruthie. Please do not encourage the children to visit.'

Then she was gone, leaving a stunned Cassie staring after her.

CHAPTER FIVE

Cassie had been feeling down for days. It wasn't that she missed the children exactly, for she didn't see all that much of them really. It was just the idea that they had been forbidden to come. That she was considered a risk to them.

She sat in the rocker in the kitchen, MacBeth on her lap. He followed her everywhere, her constant companion. They were quite wrong about him, she knew that now. Training school had taught him not to bark at other dogs and whatever had happened to Ruthie, there must have been some other explanation, for he was not a vicious dog.

She took him to the hospital with her and the children there loved him. After allowing himself to be patted and played with he would go over to the nurses' station and lie patiently under the desk until she was ready to leave. Marquis consented to sharing his home, but only on condition that he, Marquis, was boss.

MacBeth silently acknowledged the cat's superiority and never rushed to be fed first or muscle in on the hearth rug. But of Cassie's personal space, the cat had no ambitions and this was left to MacBeth alone.

Of Marc, there had been no sign. Then one day, out of the blue, two tickets arrived for a concert in town. Unsure what had prompted him to send them, she considered whether she should go or not.

It was her day at the hospital and a perfect opportunity to give the tickets away as the coming concert was the main topic of conversation among the nurses, several of whom where desperately in love with *Domino*. The staff were further thrown by the news of a large donation to the Paediatric Ward. The children's ward was in desperate need of money and the news that it was specifically for them and not to be swallowed up in other areas of the hospital came as a great relief.

All in all it was a good day and Cassie, going home in a much lighter frame of mind, decided that yes, she would go the concert. Once home, she rang her friend in the next village who was delighted to accompany her in two weeks' time to a *Domino* concert.

Leaves lay in crispy bundles down the sides of the drive and patterned the lawns, the days were shortening and winter wasn't far away the night Cassie set out to pick up her friend. Alf had been around to make sure she knew about the forthcoming concert and was delighted when he heard that she was going.

'You won't be disappointed, Mrs,' he'd said.

Barbara Thompson was a friend from early schooldays and Cassie had only recently rekindled the acquaintance. The discovery that they still had a lot in common despite Barbara's marriage and the care of two elderly relatives, was a pleasure she hadn't anticipated.

Her friend was dressed in black trousers and jacket with a white sweater and scarf. Cassie's smart red coat over a warm skirt and jumper looked overkill in comparison.

'My goodness, don't tell me it's one of those things where everyone wears black and white and falls around screaming their heads off.'

Barbara laughed. 'It's not a pop concert, it's classical and you'll love it.'

The seats were some of the best in the house and Cassie could feel her friend's eyes on her as they lowered themselves into them. When the curtains went back, the stage was bare apart from a high stool with a back rest. There didn't appear to be any backing group and the only lighting was soft and centred on the stool.

When he walked on to the stage the applause was deafening. Dressed in close fitting black trousers, white open-necked loose shirt and black waistcoat, his dark hair flat against his head, he was breathtaking. As soon as he sat down the audience stilled. You could hear yourself breathe in the silence.

When the first notes rippled across the auditorium the whole place seemed to sigh and Cassie was captivated. The performance lasted an hour then a break of fifteen minutes before the last performance which lasted three quarters of an hour. They filed out in silence and were just leaving the foyer when they were stopped by Mr Munro.

'Miss Rennington, nice to see you here. Did you enjoy the performance?'

'Very much, thank you.' She introduced her friend.

'Mr Dominic sends his regards and invites you to join him in his dressing-room.'

Startled, Cassie glanced at her friend.

Mr Munro caught the glance. 'Mrs Thompson as well, of course.'

If Barbara had been MacBeth she would have been running around panting in excitement. So, smiling, Cassie inclined her head and followed Mr Munro.

In truth, Cassie had been bowled over by Marc's playing. Now her heart was bouncing around in her chest and making her feel quite sick with anticipation.

She needn't have worried, the dressing-room was full of people, but Mr Munro cut a path through the crowds and she found herself standing next to Marc. Ignoring everyone else he smiled a welcome as though there were

45

only the two of them in the room.

Cassie caught her breath and it was only Barbara's nudging that reminded her to introduce her friend.

'You didn't tell me you knew him personally,' her friend gasped as they left the building an hour later. 'Why on earth did you turn down that offer of an invite to supper? I wouldn't have hung around, you didn't need to worry about me.'

'I didn't turn it down because of you. The invite was for both of us, I'm sure. Aftershow parties just aren't my thing. I'm sorry, did I spoil your night?'

'No, of course not. He's a wonderful performer, isn't he? How did you meet him?'

'He's my neighbour, would you believe, and he knocked down my garden wall.'

She didn't like the expression on her friend's face, nor the way she was nodding her head. Then they both laughed and for the first time Cassie admitted, 'He is rather gorgeous, isn't he?'

There was a lot more to it than that, Cassie admitted to herself later that night as she tossed and twisted in bed. When their eyes met in the dressing-room it was as if some secret message had passed between them. He had been searching for her both on the stage and off. What would he have done if she hadn't gone to the concert, but she had, and something deep down inside her told her nothing was going to be the same from now on.

She had very little sleep that night and woke tired and anxious the following morning. MacBeth demanded a walk after breakfast then he and Marquis had a spat that ended up with a very angry cat sat on top of the press. Cassie scolded both of them and tried to settle down to some of her family history when the phone rang.

When Marc's voice came through the line she nearly dropped the receiver.

'The children would like you to have dinner with us this evening.'

She felt like saying, I'm not a threat to them over there, then? Then a tiny voice whispered, would Mae have the authority to warn her off without Marc's knowledge?

There was only one way to know.

'Thank you, I'd like that.'

'See you at seven,' and the line went dead.

A monochrome day suddenly shot into Technicolor and there wasn't enough time to do everything she had to do. What do you take children who invite you to dinner? Would the children be eating at that time of evening? The only wine she had in the house was hardly suitable for a person like Marc, but did she have time to go into town, if she wanted to have a bath and wash her hair. All these questions and more scrambled for position in her head.

When seven o'clock came she had been sitting in the rocking chair ready and waiting for the past half-an-hour. The wine was wrapped and standing on the table. For the children there lay a box of homemade fudge and marzipan figures decorated with iced lacing.

Nerves were getting the upper hand as she watched the pointers of the old clock on the mantelshelf. At two minutes past she stood up and, sending MacBeth to his bed, put on her coat and, picking up the gifts, left the house. It was cold and dark as she made to walk down the drive. But then a beam of torch light to her right made her hesitate. Marc was coming through the unlocked wicket gate.

'Thought you might need a light.' Without asking he took her arm and led her down the drive. 'I'm pushing to get a street lamp down here. The nearest one to the church is outside Brown's Guest House, not much good to us, is it?'

'It would be a good idea. I haven't a torch myself. I don't usually go out at night, unless I drive.'

The light above the church door was on but not strong enough to penetrate the trees that lined her drive. She handed over the gifts which he laid to one side as he took her coat.

Then she would have gone through to the kitchen, but he opened the door across the hall. The children were all gathered in

48

the lounge dressed and seated in shining expectation. Cassie had a struggle to keep a straight face, they looked so un-natural.

Mae stood by a large Gothic fireplace, her glance never wavering from the children. Feeling like Maria, out of *The Sound Of Music*, she moved forward into the room.

'Have you brought MacBeth?' Sam wanted to know.

'The cat sits on our wall, but it won't come down,' Donald said, while casting wary glances at Mae and fingering something in his trouser pocket.

'They didn't die,' said Ruthie, while sucking her thumb.

Marc told Sam that they hadn't brought MacBeth while Cassie knelt down by the settee where Ruthie was curled up and said, 'No, Ruthie, they didn't die, they came to live with me.'

'Can I come and live with you, too?'

'Wouldn't you miss your father and brothers and sisters?'

'They could come too.'

Marc came forward and lifting the little girl in his arms carried her from the room. 'Are you sure you are going to be able to stay awake long enough to eat this dinner, Ruthie?'

'Is Cassie coming?' the tired voice asked as they all crossed the hall to the dining-room. Here, Mr Munro and the cook were waiting to serve tomato soup, sausage mash and peas and trifle for afters. Their favourite meal, Mr Munro, who had joined them for the meal, told Cassie.

Ruthie fell asleep halfway through and Douglas disgraced himself by letting a half unconscious spider out of his pocket and frightening Dorothy. Mae sat aloof throughout the meal, answering only when spoken to. Back in the lounge the older children loved the homemade sweets and then it was time for bed and Mae guided them out of the room.

Marc handed Cassie a glass of cherry brandy, her favourite, and said, 'Thank you for this evening. I realise it probably wasn't what you were expecting but the children missed you while I was away.'

Cassie looked down at the brandy swirling in the glass. She couldn't tell him that she had been warned off contact with the children, because he would want to know who by, as it obviously hadn't been him, and she couldn't see blaming Mae helping her relations with the girl.

So instead she looked up and smiled. 'It was a lovely evening. I enjoyed it very much.'

Logs crackled and hissed in the large grate, their flames and the light from the many lamps warming the stone walls of the room. Thick green carpet covered the floor and green drapes hung at narrow Gothic windows of stained glass. The deep armchairs on either side of the fireplace, where they sat, were perfect for a relaxing evening, but Cassie was feeling anything but relaxed.

'You have never been married, have you?' The question came from Marc after a spell of silent contemplation.

'No.'

'But you love children.'

'I love my career.'

'As a teacher.'

'Yes.'

'Don't you want to get married and have children of your own?'

Cassie frowned. 'I've never met anyone I wanted to marry. And neither have you, it would seem.' That should shut him up she thought, and was totally devastated by his answer.

'I was married very young and she died.'

Cassie gazed down into the nearly empty brandy glass. 'I'm sorry,' she said, before finishing off the brandy and rising to her feet.

'Please, don't,' he placed his glass on a nearby table and rising crossed the floor to take her hands in his. 'Don't go like this, I'd like you to get to know the children and come over as often as you like. Will you do that?'

She looked down at his beautiful hands, long and slim yet strong and calloused in places. When she thought of what damage he might have done to those hands chopping up the tree and building the garden wall, she shuddered. What a loss he would be to the world of music.

'Yes,' she said, refusing to look at him directly. 'But I must go now, MacBeth will be fretting.'

He led her out into the hall and helped her on with her coat. When he picked up the torch Cassie realised he wasn't going to let her go home alone. At the door of the vicarage Cassie turned to say, 'Goodnight,' but he was already halfway to the wicket gate.

CHAPTER SIX

In the days before Christmas Cassie wondered what life would have been like without Marc and the children next door. Her beautiful home was complete, she had the pets and was doing well with her family history. She loved her work at the hospital keeping the children busy, helping them with their schoolwork, listening to them read and admiring their artwork.

Marc's children were in and out of the vicarage garden now, Sam to play with MacBeth and the twins. If they weren't building dens in the orchard they were at the back door hoping to be offered pop and biscuits.

Her reactions to Marc's occasional appearances in her kitchen, she tried not to think about. In the weeks since the concert she had found it harder to ignore the attraction between them. He had begun to matter to her in a way that scared her. Did she tell him of her past, of the secret reason why she no longer worked? How would he react, she wondered.

He had lost his wife at an early age and surrounded himself with children from tragic backgrounds. A talented, successful artist, financially secure, surely he would understand where she was coming from.

As though her thoughts had conjured him up she watched him supervising the erection of the new street light at the bottom of her drive. He turned and waved when he saw her sitting in the lounge window seat. She raised a hand, then, on impulse, was hurrying through into the hall and reaching for her coat.

The workmen were finishing off when she arrived.

'How on earth did you arrange it so quickly,' she asked Marc. 'It normally takes forever to get anything done these days.'

He laughed. 'I have a music lover on the Parish Council.'

Cassie groaned. 'It wouldn't be a certain Mr Manners would it?'

'How clever of you to guess.'

They were walking arm in arm back up the drive to the house. He followed her inside and into the lounge where she offered him a drink.

'I would like you and the children to spend Christmas day with me, if that is possible?'

He gave her a strange look. 'Are you sure?'

'Of course,' she smiled hesitantly.

'Then we'd love to.'

They continued to chat and finish their drinks then he kissed her cheek before leaving. After he had gone Cassie crossed to the mirror and stared at her reflection in the glass. She wasn't a love struck teenager she chided herself, but she had a dreadful feeling she was in love. Dreadful, because she was afraid, scared of the pain that would follow should she allow herself to dream.

Cassie spent the last three days before Christmas preparing for her company. Mr Munro was roped into help raise the Christmas tree as Marc had two local concerts to prepare for. Then there was all the shopping, food preparation and present wrapping and Cassie realised she hadn't enjoyed herself so much for years.

On Christmas Eve her friend, Barbara, came over for drinks with her husband. They were too polite to say anything but Cassie could tell they were not comfortable in her beautiful home. She walked around the house after their departure complimenting herself on its style and quality while in the back of her mind she saw Barbara's lounge with its two old sofas draped in throws, the fifties style teak sideboard and the outsize television in the corner.

Magazines and newspapers were scattered over a low table and a box of toffees lay on the floor by a bag of knitting. She shrugged, closed the door and headed back to the kitchen.

Next morning with the smell of roasting turkey following her down the hall, Cassie opened the door to Marc and a group of very excited children. They all carried parcels in their hands and a chorus of greetings rang out as she welcomed them in.

Sam made for the kitchen and the sounds of a scrabbling MacBeth. Donald headed for the stairs and would have been up them like a shot but for Marc's hand on his collar. Mae was holding hands with Dorothy and Ruthie, though the little one was struggling to be free.

All were shepherded into the lounge including MacBeth and the cat to sit around the Christmas tree and cast anxious glances at the parcels piled beneath. The cat curled up on the rug in front of the fire while MacBeth gave every package a thorough sniffing.

'Shall we open them now or wait until tea time?' Cassie asked Marc.

'If we wait and take them home with us then we will not mess up Cassie's beautiful home,' Mae said.

Marc, after one startled look at Mae said, 'Yes, of course you're right.'

A howl of complaint came from Donald, and Ruthie, who had been piling the parcels they had brought amongst the others under the tree, said, 'But I wanted to see Cassie open hers.'

'Of course you do,' said Cassie bending down and taking the little girl's hand, 'and if you come with me we will find a bag big enough to put all the wrappers in.' So after indicating that Marc should help himself to a drink she left the room with Ruthie and a cross cat that was not impressed by the disruption.

Halfway through the present-giving Cassie saw Mae say something to Marc. Laughing, Marc called a halt to the proceedings. 'Enough for now kids, Mae is reminding us that we have a surprise for Cassie.' Donald grumbled and Sam didn't look too pleased but both left the tree and came to stand by their father.

Mae left the room and returned with one of Marc's guitars. Sitting at Marc's knee she began to sing. Softly Marc accompanied her.

She's beautiful, Cassie thought, then while she listened to the love song she watched the girl's face and realised with a shock that Mae loved him. At eighteen this was no child but a woman in love and the knowledge sent a savage pain through her heart.

Now it was the children's turn and Cassie sat through their performance with a lump in her throat. After which she made her excuses and hurried to the kitchen. The turkey had been cooked and carved, the vegetables were in their serving dishes, as were the sauces and side dishes. All was placed into the heated trolley and wheeled through into the dining room.

Mae came forward to help dish up the children's servings.

'You have a beautiful voice, Mae, are you going to be trained professionally?'

She bent her small finely boned face over the plates. 'No, Marc needs me.'

'It would be a pity to waste such a wonderful voice, I'm surprised Marc doesn't insist you do something with it.'

The girl looked up then and Cassie nearly spilt the sauce she was serving at the venomous look she saw in the dark almond eyes.

'I will always be there for Marc,' she stated.

The meal was a success but they had no sooner left the table than little Ruthie was sick.

'I told you it would be too much for her,' Mae spoke quietly to Marc.

Then Sam, who had insisted on taking his plate to the kitchen, fell over MacBeth and broke the plate. It was one of a Shelley dinner service which Marc immediately offered to pay for. How could she explain to him that it was a very old design unavailable today? She bit back her disappointment and proceeded to lead the children in a game.

Donald wanted to play hide and seek but Marc forbade it.

'Why, it's a nice big house, there will be lots

of places to hide, won't there, Cassie?'

Cassie hesitated, not wanting them running all over her beautiful house, heaven only knew what damage they could do.

Mae said, 'Why don't you open the rest of the presents then it will be time to go home.'

'Yes,' the twins chorused, charging back to the tree, game forgotten.

Cassie glanced towards Marc who gave her a smile and nod of the head.

'Good idea,' he said.

For Cassie there was a silk scarf from Mae, a tartan collar for MacBeth from Sam, a box of chocolates from the twins and from the now wide awake Ruthie a silver bangle, 'Just like mine,' she whispered in Cassie's ear.

From Marc there was a delicate silk jacket, quilted and embroidered with multi coloured dominoes. She kissed all the little ones as they left, even a reluctant Donald, until there was only herself and Marc left in the hall. Then he took her in his arms and kissed her on the mouth. With a catch in his throat he murmured, 'Thank you.' And left.

*   *   *

The family next door were visiting America for the New Year. Cassie had stayed at the hospital as long as was practicable on New Year's Eve. Driving home through the dark cold evening with sleet hammering across the windscreen she was looking forward to the warmth of the house and her welcome from MacBeth and Marquis.

When the black shape appeared suddenly in front of her she jammed on the brakes. A dull thud and a jar that threw her forward against the seat belt. Nothing moved in the following silence but for the persistent rattle of strengthening hail stones.

The shower passed and Cassie, once she knew there was no harm to herself, considered climbing out to see what it was she had driven into. The large shape was still there unmoving. No one appeared out of the darkness which made her nervous. Cautiously she opened the door and climbed out on to the dark road. There was no other traffic in sight.

The object blocking her way was a dark coloured lorry standing without lights at the side of the road. She moved up to the cabin and rapped loudly on the door. It was all dark inside and there was no response. Raising herself on her toes she tried to see inside the cabin but it was too high. After another thump on the door still raised no reply she reached up and opened the door. The cabin was empty.

Back in her own car, hissing and spitting about irresponsible people, wasn't it illegal to leave a vehicle on the road side with no lights showing, she switched the engine on and tried to reverse. There was a metallic tearing sound and with a shudder the little car tore free.

Determined to report the incident the minute she arrived home she edged past the lorry and continued on her way.

Home at last, she lent back against the closed door and watched the animals rushing to greet her. Shocked to find herself shaking she bent down to pick up MacBeth and crush him to her. He covered her chin with a wet tongue and when she went to wipe her hand across her face she discovered tears.

Placing the dog back on the floor she went through into the kitchen and sitting down in the rocking chair dropped her face into her hands and wept.

Much later she tried to ring the police station but the lines were busy and in the end she just gave up and went to bed.

CHAPTER SEVEN

On the second of January it was all over the newspapers. The lorry had been carrying illegal immigrants when the vehicle broke down and the driver panicked. He had set forty-seven people, men, women and children loose in the countryside and scarpered. Thirty-five had been rounded up by the police but twelve were still missing and they were asking the public's help in finding them. The driver was yet to be traced.

'Well,' Cassie spoke to MacBeth, the dog waiting patiently to be fed any leftover scraps from breakfast, 'there won't be much point in phoning the police now, will there. We had better go and see what damage poor Daffodil suffered.'

When she opened the front door MacBeth ran past her and dashed across the lawn to water the trees. Alf's head popped up on the other side of the car and gave Cassie a bit of a shock.

'Alf, what can I do for you?'

He lifted his cap and scratched beneath it. 'I think it might be what I can do for you, Mrs. I see you've had a bit of a bump, not too bad mind, but I think the other fella must have come off worst. See it's just a case of getting this bump out and taking these scratches off,' he said, coming around to the front of the car.

Cassie felt in need of more coffee. She looked around for the little white van and saw it parked down by the gate. 'How did you know I'd had an accident, Alf?'

'Oh I didn't, Mrs. I was coming to see if you wanted those trees of yours doctoring seeing as how they hang right over the road. The council will be on to you if you don't do something about them.'

'Do you never take any time off, Alf?'

'Oh yes, Mrs, we've had a grand two days, and you?'

'Very quiet, Alf, but you go ahead and do

whatever needs doing.'

'And the car?'

'Yes, the car as well, but you won't have it away too long, will you, I'll need it for the hospital on Monday.'

Alf grinned like a naughty gnome. 'I'll just get my stuff and it'll be done in a wink.'

Cassie was left gaping after him as he trotted down the drive. Then shaking her head she retreated back into the house.

Three days later, Marc and his family were back from the States. Cassie had thought no more about the incident of the immigrants. Alf had been as good as his word and Daffodil was no worse for the bump. He was busy that morning sawing away at the overhanging branches of the trees at the bottom of the garden.

The first she knew of Dominic's return was the twins and Sam standing on her back doorstep. MacBeth went mad, jumping up at Sam and threatening to bowl him over. The twins were in the kitchen without waiting for an invite and sitting at the table waiting for pop and biscuits.

'I was sick in the airplane,' complained Dorothy.

'That was because it was bumpy and we had to keep our seatbelts on. It nearly crashed when the lightning hit us. It dropped down sudden like this,' and he demonstrated with his arms flaying. 'A woman in the next seat had her handbag on her knee and it flew up and hit her in the face. Served her right because you're not supposed to have anything on your knee. Then a man's nose started to bleed and wouldn't stop, there was blood all down the front of him and the lady gave him tissues and they were soaked straight away, it was ages before it stopped.'

He was really into his story now and the more carried away he became the greener Dorothy became.

So Cassie called a halt and thrust a biscuit at him.

'Marc told everyone about you and your house,' Dorothy spoke shyly.

'Me?'

She nodded. 'Yes, all the time and Mae got real mad.'

'I'm sure she wouldn't be cross because of what Marc was saying, perhaps certain parties were being naughty, it's not easy looking after so many you know.'

'I told you,' mumbled Donald between a mouth full of biscuit. 'Told you she wouldn't believe you.'

Turning away, Cassie frowned as she stood looking out over the sink to the garden. Had Marc really talked about her to people? What had he said, she wondered? She worried about the girl Mae as well, was Marc aware of the girl's feelings for him?

The twins were arguing and she turned back

to the table.

In town a few days later she noticed Mae climbing into a taxi with a rather strange looking man. Standing in front of a shop window she watched them mirrored in the glass. The taxi pulled away, taking them out of the town in the opposite direction to the village.

All the way home she worried about whether or not she should mention Mae's behaviour to Marc. It really was none of her business, but she couldn't help fret about the girl. Who was the man she had been with and where had they gone, did Marc know?

Back home she tried to put it out of her mind. But it persisted to the point that she could settle to nothing else. When she thought the time was right for Mae to have returned she dreamt up an excuse about running out of milk and walked next door.

James Munro answered the door. 'Ah, Miss Cassie, come along in. It's a rare cold night outside.'

She was shown into the kitchen which seemed to be the heart of everything. Here Mrs O'Connor was just on the point of leaving, but as Cassie hesitantly offered her excuse she left what she was doing and disappearing around the door of an enormous fridge came back with a bottle of milk.

The children were in the conservatory, but there was no sign of Mae. James Munro had

64

taken himself off, so Cassie quietly asked Mrs O'Connor, 'Mae not around tonight?'

'That will be all, Mrs O'Connor, you can go now.' Mae's quiet authority chilled Cassie. She spun round to face the girl's hostility.

'Did you wish to speak to me?'

'I saw you getting into a taxi in town earlier today and I was worried about your safety, that's all.'

Mae's eyes narrowed, emphasising their almond shape. 'My safety or otherwise is none of your concern, Miss Rennington.'

'I realise that now, I'm sorry I intruded.'

She had started to leave when Mae spoke again, 'I suppose you will now carry your tale to Marc.'

Annoyed, Cassie turned back to face the girl. 'I never tell tales, Mae.' Then she left.

There was no chemist in the village so when Cassie came down with a feverish cold and it was one of the days for the part time surgery which had a dispensary, she decided to attend.

The waiting room was tiny and people obligingly shuffled along the bench to accommodate her. A low table cluttered with magazines stood in the centre of the room and a box of children's toys under the one window that looked out on to a brick wall. A fluorescent tube sizzled overhead casting an unreal light over the waiting people.

The door to the doctor's room clicked open and a nurse appeared in the doorway. The

65

previous patient passed her and without glancing into the room headed for the street door. With a genuine smile on her face the nurse called out the name of the next patient.

Cassie watched Mae's departure with a frown. Something was happening here, something she was sure Marc should know about. On her way home with a bottle of cough medicine safely tucked into her bag she stopped outside the church and contemplated Marc's reaction should she attempt to inform him of her worries about Mae.

Alf intruded into her thoughts. 'I've just finished, Mrs. The lads'll be along later to clear the rubbish.'

'Oh right, if you come up to the house with me I'll pay you now.'

'Righty oh, I'll just lock up the van.'

He waited at the front door while Cassie went through into the kitchen to collect his money, waiting for him in an envelope on the mantle.

'Right carry on next door,' he said as he took the envelope from her.

Cassie didn't normally gossip but Alf was a fountain of information and she wondered if it had anything to do with Mae: 'Oh yes?' she said, inviting his confidence.

He nodded his head. 'Oldest one turned up the other night with her whole family in tow. Rumour has it they're illegals, aren't they, given poor Marc a hell of a fix.'

'I thought she was an orphan with no family, why else would Marc adopt her?'

Alf was shaking his head. 'She was a twelve-year-old bar girl when he found her. She saved his life when he was set on by thugs in a back alley one night, that's what he told me. Said her life would have been in danger if he'd left her there without protection.'

'What will he do now?'

Alf shrugged his shoulders. 'Don't know, Mrs, but I wouldn't want his problem.'

Cassie watched him walk back down the drive before closing the door and making her way thoughtfully back to the kitchen. She saw the police car from the front bedroom window the next morning. Two minutes later a second car pulled up.

You have finished dusting, go back downstairs, she told herself, but curiosity drew her back to the window and a short while later she saw several people being bundled into the cars.

A tearful Mae stood on the steps with Marc's comforting arm around her. She swallowed the lump that had grown in her throat, and picking up polish and duster hurried down the stairs.

That afternoon a wrapped up Sam was playing with MacBeth in the garden when there was a rap on the back door and Marc entered. Tall and dark he stood framed in the light from the window. He started to say something then took two strides forward and she was in his arms. After a long kiss he said, 'I missed you like the very devil.'

She broke away and stood before the roaring fire in the old range. 'I missed you too, all of you.' She had felt the stress in him and hoped he would talk about Mae.

'Is something wrong?'

She turned to him smiling. 'No, are you home for a while now?'

'Yes,' he said with a frown, 'I have some things to sort out here then my next concert isn't until the beginning of March.'

'A drink?' she offered.

The frown continued to crease his brow as he accepted. Their conversation thereafter consisted of smalltalk and he left without ever mentioning Mae. Cassie was disappointed to say the least. She had hoped that their new found relationship would include sharing, but then she acknowledged that her own past still hid in the shadows.

CHAPTER EIGHT

When next Cassie met Mae, the girl crossed the street to avoid her. This is ridiculous, she thought and deliberately went after her. She caught up to her at the church gates.

'Mae, unless you want me to come in and

include Marc in our conversation please stop and listen to what I have to say.'

The girl turned and looked down at her from halfway up the steps leading to the front door. 'I have nothing to say to you, my uncle and his family are in a terrible place because of you.'

Cassie stepped back in shock. 'Because of me?'

'You crashed into their vehicle and told the police where they could be found.'

Cassie shook her head. 'That's not true, any of it. I bumped into a stationary vehicle, yes, but it was empty and I never said a word to the police.'

'You were seen and now my uncle cannot stay here, and cannot go home because China will not have them back, they will be always homeless.'

'Mae, you must believe me, I had nothing to do with this thing, and whatever you think I am not your enemy, I would like very much to be your friend.'

Mae gave a laugh that belonged to a woman older and harder than the girl standing on the steps, then she disappeared inside and shut the door.

Cassie hired a solicitor to make enquiries as to the position of the Choo family, only to be told that Marc had gone down the same path and been unsuccessful. So for the time being she gave up on Mae and concentrated on the younger members of the family.

Ruthie still wanted to come and live with her and never missed a chance to follow the boys into her garden.

Marc was also a frequent visitor and would settle into her kitchen with the comfort of a second home. She was surprised one day to discover that he gave impromptu concerts at music nights at the 'Green Man'. He invited her to join him at the next event and it wasn't until later that she found out from Donald that Marc was in the habit of taking Mae along on these occasions.

Her mother had always warned that bad things came in threes and she was certainly right in this case. First the issue of the dog, then the immigrant family, now she was to play gooseberry at their musical evening. No wonder the girl thought she was public enemy number one.

On the night in question she dithered between going and making the best of it or sending some excuse and backing out. In the end she dressed as quietly as possible in a sober grey skirt and jumper under a houndstooth checked coat, tall black boots and black kid gloves.

When she arrived in front of the church Marc was standing at the top of the steps. He ran down to greet her and tucking her arm in his guided her back on to the pavement.

'Where is Mae, isn't she coming? Donald

said she always accompanied you.'

He laughed. 'She's already gone. There's a chap there from a record company wants to hear her sing.'

Cassie stopped in her tracks. 'But surely she's too good to be singing in a pub. You can't possibly approve.'

'She's nearly nineteen, what do you think I should do, forbid her? I played my way round pubs for two years at her age. I have tried getting her to go to music college but she won't budge.'

Cassie glanced at his profile in the light of a street lamp. 'You do know she's in love with you, don't you?'

'Of course she loves me, I'm her guardian.'

'Oh, I think you know you are much more than that to her.'

'What on earth do you mean?' he asked, coming to a halt beside her.

'She's not a girl, Marc, she's a woman and she's in love with you.'

He shook his head. 'She may think she is but she'll find out the difference when she meets someone her own age.'

They continued on their way and soon came to the 'Green Man'. It was crowded, the musical nights very popular, but quickly Marc found them a seat at the side of a raised platform that passed as a stage.

Marc left to get them drinks and shortly after Cassie felt someone's gaze on her and lifting her head looked around. There were several people with a variety of musical instruments propped alongside them. Alf waved to her from across the room, and she recognised James Munro propping up the bar.

A shiver rose from her feet to the hair on the back of her neck as her glance clashed with Mae's. The girl was sitting on the edge of the platform with a short bearded man who was talking rapidly. As though sensing his partner's distraction he looked up to follow her glance. Cassie turned away as Marc returned to the table with their drinks.

*　　*　　*

By nine o'clock the place was so full Cassie didn't believe they could squeeze one more person in. The music started when an elderly man stood up and began to play an Irish jig on his fiddle. People clapped and stamped in time to the tune and he'd only barely finished when a middle aged, well-padded woman stood up and began to sing a lilting ballad.

There was more fiddle music then Mae rose to her feet and her sweet rendering of *Love is a Many Splendoured Thing* nearly brought the house down. This was followed by a young lad on the Northumberland pipes and by the time he was finished playing *The Skye Boat Song* there was hardly a dry eye to be seen.

Cassie was enjoying herself immensely when

Marc picked up his guitar and hitching himself on to the platform began to strum the instrument. Laughter and chatter faded away, Marc smiled, glanced across at Cassie and began to play. Feeling an ache deep in her chest Cassie closed her eyes and let the music wash around her until she was quite alone in that overcrowded room.

When she opened her eyes Mae was standing by Marc, her voice melding beautifully with his music. Suddenly it was all too much and rising to her feet she sidled away from the table and headed for the ladies'.

* * *

Last year's hard work came to fruition when first the snowdrops then the crocuses popped their pretty heads above ground. Not long after there was a heavy snowfall and Cassie fretted that she might lose the lot, but no sooner had the snow began to melt than their little heads appeared again. Now it was March and there were daffodils, miniature iris and early tulips to complement the others.

Marc had left in the first week of March on a six week tour of Europe. He rang her up three or four times a week and she found herself waiting for his calls more and more as time passed. Once again Mae had banned the children from coming to visit and Cassie was thrown back on her own company. Barbara, her friend in the next village, was having domestic problems and unavailable for the present time.

She wandered the house looking for small imperfections, different coloured cushions on a settee, or the need of a plant, or lamp in an exposed corner. The woman from the village had turned out to be very obliging and a good worker. So apart from personal laundry and the occasional washing of china and ornaments, the house practically ran itself.

The family history that had occupied her in the early days had come to a halt at a seemingly insurmountable problem and she had yet to venture into another branch of the tree.

She increased her two days at the hospital to four and it was while encouraging a group of children in their maths on a Tuesday morning that a little girl came down from emergency and was put into an empty bed at the top of the ward. Normally this would have attracted only a passing glance from Cassie, but the shock of seeing Mae following the trolley to the bedside made Cassie rise to her feet and excusing herself from the children hurry up the ward.

'Mae, what is it, what's wrong?'

Mae gave her an angry look. 'There is nothing wrong. Ruthie is feeling unwell. I am being careful, that is all.' And she turned her back cutting Cassie off from the bed.

When the staff nurse left Cassie followed her back to the desk.

'Excuse me, but can you tell me what is wrong with Ruthie?'

The nurse looked surprised. 'Do you know her, Cassie?'

'They're my neighbours, the father's away and I just wondered if . . .'

'We're waiting for Mr Parker to come down. She's complaining of a sore head and her neck hurts her when she moves,' she glanced hesitantly at Cassie as though deciding whether to say more or not. 'She also has a rash.'

Cassie swallowed hard. 'You suspect meningitis?'

'We don't deal in suspicions, Cassie. Mr Parker will be down shortly then we'll see.'

Back in the ward, two more nurses were around the restless little girl while Mae stood at the end of the bed looking on. Cassie went back to the children, quieting them by reading a story. She saw the consultant come on to the ward and watched out of the corner of her eye as he examined Ruthie, then talked first to Mae then to the staff nurse as they moved back to the station together.

After a while she closed the book and leaving the children to draw pictures about the story she went back to the nurses' station to ask after Ruthie.

'It's probably an allergy, it's definitely not

meningitis,' the nurse said.

'Will she be sent home?'

'Not yet, it's a bad attack and we want to find out exactly what caused it.'

At lunch time Mae left the ward and Cassie, on the point of going for her own lunch, stopped by Ruthie's bed.

'Hello Ruthie, how are you feeling now?'

'Cassie, my tummy hurts, can I come and stay with you?'

'No darling, you have to stay in the hospital until your tummy gets better.'

'But my head's better now,' and tears welled in the large blue eyes. Taking the little hand in her own Cassie said, 'Would you like me to stay with you until Mae returns?'

'Uhuh.'

'Would you like me to read you a story?'

'About MacBeth.'

'You want me to tell you a story?'

'Uhuh.'

So Cassie began to form into a story all the funny things the little dog had done in the past few days and soon Ruthie had fallen asleep.

Cassie tried to leave but two fingers of her hand were trapped tightly in the small fist so she sat down again and watched her sleep. Was this what was missing in her life, she wondered.

Had she allowed past nightmares to dictate only an empty future? Wasn't that what she wanted, no more fear, no more hurt, no more pain? Only the dream, to go back, back into a time of safety and security where there had been love and warmth. A thumb had found its way to the soft mouth and the sound of unconscious sucking could be heard.

She came to with a start. Mae was standing beside her, brows drawn down in a frown. 'What are you doing here?'

Ruthie woke and started to cry.

'Now look what you have done, please go away.'

Cassie eased her fingers from the little hand and stood up.

Mae made to sit down in her place but Ruthie wanted Cassie.

'Ruthie behave yourself. Cassie must go home now. She has all those animals to look after.'

Ruthie's tears ceased. 'Will you come back?'

Cassie nodded, smiled and left.

$$* \qquad * \qquad *$$

That night Marc phoned and Cassie told him about Ruthie's scare.

'I'll be home on the next flight.'

'No, really Marc there's no panic. The doctors are convinced it is an allergy, it's just a matter of finding out what she is allergic to.'

'The last concert is in Paris tomorrow night. I'll be home on Thursday. Take care of her for me. I don't understand why Mae didn't ring me.'

'She wouldn't want to worry you once she knew it wasn't anything really bad.'

'I suppose not. I've missed you, Cassie, I hope we can get together when I get back?'

'I've missed you too and the children.'

'See you soon then.'

Cassie was working on Thursday and the first she saw of Marc was when he walked on to the ward just after lunch to collect Ruthie, who was much better and ready to go home. Cassie had offered to have Ruthie play with the other children, but Mae would not allow it and Ruthie was made to sit on her bed and wait for her father.

When Marc arrived the little girl rushed to his side where she was plucked up into his arms. After a few words with Mae and a curious glance at Cassie the trio left. Cassie had been prepared for a welcome and was deeply concerned when he left without a word.

That evening she sat in the kitchen and waited for a call, a knock on the door, some word to show that he had meant what he had said on all those night time phone calls. She prepared and ate a dinner of baked salmon with broccoli and lemon sauce, washed her dishes, watched the news on television, and waited. By ten-thirty she was ready for bed, made herself a hot drink and waited.

CHAPTER NINE

Next morning she dismissed the cleaner, packed a bag for herself and food for the animals. Then she cornered Marquis and pushed him into a cat basket. The bags were placed in Daffodil's boot, the cat on the back seat and MacBeth without permission seated himself in the passenger seat.

Now they were ready to go. She had no idea where she was heading, it seemed sensible to go south into warmer climes but after a while they were travelling north. Finding accommodation not only for herself but the animals as well might present her with a problem and she thought about this as she drove.

They ended up in a log cabin by a lakeside a short walk into a small village surrounded by wonderful countryside. Walks were many and varied and after the first day Marquis insisted on accompanying them everywhere. They walked in a line, MacBeth first then Cassie and lastly the cat at a more leisurely pace.

Cassie ate at the village inn with MacBeth beneath the table, while Marquis sat on the wall outside and waited for them, then together they would stroll back to the lodge. She called the hospital on the second day and told them she would be away for a few days

79

and that she wasn't quite sure when she would be back, but she would let them know.

Cassie had been teaching for four years when she met the languages teacher who stole her heart. He was every woman's dream come true and within a few short weeks they were married. They were madly in love and at first while the flame of passion burned bright, everything was perfect.

Then the dream turned and became a nightmare as friends tried to warn her about other women and the possibility of a wife in France. Debts crawled out from the shadows and the good life began to fray around the edges. When asked about the French wife, he'd simply shrugged it off.

In the end she left him and life became a bit of a struggle then, one day, a lottery ticket provided her with unlimited funds. She was rich, she was free. But she wasn't, for within a few days of her win he was back, insisting that he would divorce the French wife and make their union legal. When she refused either to have him back or hand over half her winnings, he'd pushed her to one side in his anger and frustration to get out and slammed the door behind him.

She was older and wiser now, but it would appear still vulnerable, she had thought to have learnt her lesson never to trust anyone with her heart again, yet here she was crying into her soup like the 'mock turtle' as her mother would have said. On the fifth day she decided to go home.

Once home, MacBeth and Marquis dashed off into the garden and soon the sound of children's voices brought her to the bedroom window. Sam and Ruthie were playing with the dog. Cassie returned to her unpacking then back downstairs to the kitchen. Here the twins were sat at the table awaiting their pop and biscuits.

She poured the pop and brought the tin of biscuits to the table. 'Where have you been?' Donald wanted to know.

'On holiday.'

'We thought you'd gone for good,' Dorothy said, picking out a biscuit with a 'thank you'.

'People don't normally take their pets on holiday with them,' Donald said.

'They do sometimes,' Dorothy intervened.

'No they don't silly, that's what they have boarding kennels and catteries for.'

'The animals had a lovely time,' Cassie interrupted before it came to a full blown argument.

'Everyone's been cross since you left,' grumbled Donald.

Dorothy was nodding her head, like a wise old sage.

'Marc is very cross with Mae,' Dorothy said in a hushed voice.

'Ruthie spilled,' pronounced Donald. 'Said you looked after her in hospital, not Mae.'

Cassie was shocked. It was true that she had taken Ruthie under her wing whenever Mae wasn't around, reading her stories and staying late to sing her to sleep at night, but Mae had been there every day.

Had Mae told Marc differently, was that why he had failed to contact her the night he brought Ruthie home? She wanted to hear more from the children but knew she couldn't ask them to gossip. She must be patient, if Mae had been found out in a lie, then surely he would be around to clarify the situation.

Children and dog came in from the garden and Cassie was kept too busy to worry.

*   *   *

The next two days passed without any sign of Marc, and Cassie tried to concentrate on other things. Telling herself she had a good life, a beautiful home, work she loved, the pets for company and the borrowed children from next door, what more could she ask for.

Mae was scolding the twins for pulling daffodils that Cassie had planted just the previous autumn. She hadn't seen Cassie, who was down on her knees preparing a summer bed further up the garden.

'They're not for you, they're for Cassie,' Donald was shouting.

Cassie pulled off her gardening gloves and stood up. Mae saw her now and made to grab the children.

'It's all right, really. I'll put them in a vase and they'll look very nice in the window.'

Donald handed over the flowers then he and his sister tore off across the garden. Cassie and Mae were left standing face to face. Mae turned to follow the twins but Cassie spoke out. 'You have nothing to worry about from me, Mae, please don't be angry.'

The girl turned her head and gave Cassie a look so full of hate that Cassie fell back. 'You think to take Marc from me,' she spoke in a quiet, flat voice, but none the less threatening for all that, 'but you will not, I will kill you first.' Then she was gone.

Cassie wasn't sure what to make of it all. That Mae was jealous was obvious and acceptable even if unnecessary, but that she should hate with such a passion was, Cassie admitted to herself, scary to say the least. She turned to go back to her gardening and found Marc coming across the lawn towards her.

'Do you have a minute?'

Her heart skipped a beat but she nodded her head. 'Would you like to go inside?'

'Thank you.' He looked harassed, his overlong hair was unkempt and his eyes were puffy and dull. He followed her into the kitchen where Cassie put on the kettle before sitting down in the rocking chair, leaving him to straddle one of the chairs from around the table.

'I have asked Mae to come and apologise to you for her recent behaviour. That she flatly refuses to do so I cannot for the world understand. So I have come to apologise on her behalf.'

Cassie stared into the fire. 'Why don't you understand, Marc. Mae is a woman in love and, rightly or wrongly, she believes me to be her rival. Her feelings for you are very strong.'

He ran his fingers through his hair making it stand up worse than ever. 'I talked to her about that after you mentioned the possibility on the night of the music venue at the "Green Man". She was really sensible about it.'

'Of course she was, you aren't her enemy, I am.'

'What on earth are we going to do? I've been scared to death to come over here after you disappeared like that, and then, when the children told me what had been happening I felt so damn stupid for believing everything Mae said. But she's always been so honest and reliable.' He shook his head in despair. 'Ruthie never stopped talking about you and I missed you. Will you accept our apology?'

'You have nothing to apologise for and Mae can't help her feelings.'

The chair creaked as he rose from it to stand alongside Cassie's rocker. 'Then I'll leave you in peace.'

'Goodnight, you can see yourself out.'

The door closed softly behind him.

CHAPTER TEN

The children were crying and shouting, but Cassie was afraid to look over her shoulder. Now Mae was there in front of her with a knife in her hand and a terrible look on her face. Cassie spun round, Marc was watching, she flung out her arms and was falling, falling. She woke up with a jerk, groped for the lamp by her bed, switched on the light and lay trembling in the aftermath of the dream.

It was Sunday and Barbara had rung to ask her out for lunch.

'We could meet at the "Black Bull" and stroll along the riverbank later.'

'I'd like that, thanks, Barbara, twelve-thirty then.'

Half-an-hour later the phone rang again. It was Marc. 'Any chance I could take you out to dinner this evening?'

On the point of saying she already had an arrangement for lunch she changed her mind and found herself accepting his offer.

She ate sparingly at lunch and listened attentively while on their walk as Barbara unburdened all her problems with elderly parents, a wayward son and a husband who refused to help.

Later that evening she had a bath, washed

her hair and spent a crazy half hour deciding what to wear. There was a green jersey dress with long sleeves and a scoop neck. Being dark with eyes as changeable as the sea, her father had said, she suited bright colours. Blue two piece in a satin cord or a choice of three red outfits.

With time closing fast and the pile on the bed mounting she found a purple suit with a three-quarter jacket and ankle length skirt. Black accessories and a long purple coat with grey lining and she was ready. Marc rang the bell on the front door and when she opened it presented her with an orchid corsage which he insisted on pinning on before escorting her to his waiting Jaguar.

Dinner was at a fashionable country club, a very exclusive, expensive place, and Cassie itched to tell him how much she detested the venue, haunted as she was by evenings spent with Greg in similar venues during his high flying days when 'living life to the full' had been his motto and she in her ignorance had followed.

'You aren't enjoying this a bit, are you?'

She looked up swiftly. 'I'm sorry?'

'You were far away, and not somewhere nice by your expression.'

She glanced down at her untouched Parma ham rolls and melon balls on a bed of lettuce. 'It's one of my favourites, honest.' And she started to eat.

Chicken in white wine followed, then making an excuse against dessert they finished off their meal with coffee and home made sweets.

They were both silent on the ride home. After a while Marc pulled on to the grass verge and switched off the engine. 'What is it, Cassie? What's really wrong?'

'I'm worried about Mae, that's all.'

Marc sat sideways on, watching her profile against the dark window. 'Mae will have to learn to accept the inevitable, that's all. Mae aside, I thought we had some kind of mutual attraction going on here.'

Cassie turned her head to look at him. 'So did I.'

'What happened?'

'Mae happened.'

'You can't seriously believe I have any feelings for Mae other than as a parent.' He sounded genuinely shocked.

'Of course not,' she said, turning back to gaze out of the window.

'Then I don't understand.'

'You believed her.'

He opened his mouth to say something, then closed it, nodding his head as he recognised where she was coming from. 'She's my daughter.' It wasn't a plea, just a statement.

'Of course,' was all she said.

The next day it was once more warm enough to sit out in the garden. The sunshine had brought out the flowers early that year and though it was still cold in the shade there had been no frost for several days. Cassie was waiting for the appearance of the children. The cat lay curled up on the windowsill and MacBeth sat at her feet.

At the sound of their voices the dog's head came up, then he was on his feet and away across the lawn. The twins were first and fighting as they came through the vestry gate. Then gentle Sam with Ruthie in tow. The cat silently jumped down from the sill and made his way indoors.

Donald had won the argument and was handing her a letter. The twins and Ruthie gathered round wanting to know what it said. The letter was a typed invitation to Sam's birthday party.

Weather permitting it would be a barbecue with games and fireworks. They all glanced round to where Sam was trying to persuade MacBeth to beg.

'It's a secret,' whispered Ruthie.

'He doesn't know,' confirmed Donald.

Cassie smiled. 'Well then I had better write my reply.'

'You will come won't you?' Ruthie asked anxiously.

'I'd love to come.'

Once she had left the children playing in the garden and returned to the house, she wasn't so sure that going to the party was such a good idea. Then she thought of little Ruthie and knew that whatever happened she couldn't disappoint the child.

On the night of the party Cassie wrapped the framed portrait of MacBeth across the corner of which was written 'to Sam with love' and a paw print. She smiled as she tied a large red bow around it.

The children had every conceivable toy and game she could think of and this idea had come to her on the spur of a moment when she had been studying some portraits in a shop window in town. MacBeth had been a very good sitter and in no time at all it had been done.

The party was in full swing when she arrived. There were several children she didn't know and she assumed the adults were their parents. Mae was organising a treasure hunt. Cassie lay her present alongside others on a table by the conservatory door and wandering inside was grateful for the drink offered by a beaming Mrs O'Connor.

Marc broke away from two fashionably dressed women and came through the conservatory to her side.

'I'm glad you came, please come and meet some of the neighbours with me.' He took her arm and led her back out into the garden. It wasn't long before she sensed Mae watching.

It broke her concentration on what Marc was saying so when he turned to her for confirmation, she was helpless and stumbled through her reply. As they walked away amused and sympathetic glances followed them.

'I sounded foolish, I'm sorry. I think I should leave now. Please tell Sam I came.'

'You can't go yet,' he said, and taking her hand led her back into the house. 'You'll miss the firework display. You've never seen the rest of the house, have you? Come and see my studio.' It was a tower room off the first floor landing and he led her inside and closed the door.

A bare room with a high ceiling and wood floor. There were gold and silver award discs on the wall and trophies on the narrow ledges of three slit windows. Several guitars stood propped against the wall. A piano and a table were the only dominant pieces of furniture in the room. He offered her the piano stool then taking off his jacket and laying it on the top of the piano he picked up an instrument and began to strum.

The sun was dying, its last rays sliding through the narrow windows to spotlight the player against the white stone walls, a troubadour from a long ago time. Cassie felt the music entering her soul, so beautiful and sad that tears were trembling on her lids when he put the guitar aside and lifting her from the stool kissed her long and hungrily.

As he released her she turned her head.

Mae stood perfectly still in the open doorway. 'Some of our guests are asking for you, Marc,' she announced like a society wife that had caught her husband misbehaving.

'I didn't hear you knock,' Marc said.

Mae flinched visibly but held her ground.

'We'll be down in a moment.' He dismissed her.

When she had gone he turned back to Cassie. 'I'm sorry I didn't realise just what a problem she'd become.'

Cassie laid a hand on his arm and smiled. 'Thank you for the music.'

'There will always be music for us, Cassie, when you care to listen.'

Blue eyes stared into grey ones for a long time then Cassie said, 'I'll be listening.'

'Then I think I had better get back to my guests.'

Cassie stayed for the firework display and to see Sam open his presents. She was pleased to see his expression of excitement when he opened the portrait of MacBeth.

'That's different,' Marc whispered in her ear.

Marc was leaving for a concert in London the next day. They had arranged to meet the day after and talk to Mae together. Cassie was at the hospital that afternoon when an emergency call came through. Ambulances were bringing in four children with smoke inhalation and burns.

Cassie kept to one side in these situations as the ward became a hive of activity. But to her horror she found herself thrown into the midst of this emergency when she recognised not one but all of Marc's children being stretchered in with oxygen masks on their faces. Last of all came Mae straight through into the ICU.

CHAPTER ELEVEN

In the corridor she bumped into a stained and harassed looking James Munro. 'Lassie, can you tell me how the bairns are,' he pleaded.

'James, what happened?' She took his hands which were shaking and tugged him to sit down next to her.

'I don't rightly ken, a box of fireworks left over from last night exploded, why or how, no-one knows. The bairns were in their rooms on their computers an' such. I was reading in my room and Mrs O'Connor had just left when there was a noise from downstairs.'

He wiped a hand across his brow leaving a dirty smut behind. 'I didn't think much on it, until I heard the lassie cry out.'

His voice shook with emotion as he continued. 'I came out of my room and smoke swept in past me. The wee lassie had Ruthie in her arms and was dragging her leg as she struggled to get the child to safety. I could see there was something wrong with her but she was calling to the others to follow her. By now we were all coughing and choking. I grabbed the other children and we struggled through the smoke and down the stairs.'

Here he let out a great sigh. 'Mae had fallen and she begged me to get the children out, which I did and called for help. But oh God help me I could nay get back inside to help Mae. Then help came and they got her out, I know she's hurt bad, lassie, what can I do?'

'Does Marc know?'

He shook his head and Cassie could see he was too upset to think straight.

'Do you have a number for him?' she asked gently.

'Aye, I do, it's on this contraption,' he said, pulling a mobile phone from his pocket. His hands shook as he handed it over.

'I'll contact Marc then we'll go and get you a cup of tea.'

'I cannot go anywhere, I was told to wait here, the police want to talk to me.'

'Then they can come and talk to you in the canteen. For the moment I have to go outside to use this phone, it's not allowed in here.'

She headed outside wondering what on earth she was going to say to Marc. The phone rang and rang but remained unanswered. He must be rehearsing she told herself, she would ring again soon, but now she must get back to

93

the children.

A policeman was standing talking to James as she passed him in the corridor and hurried back to the ward. The twins were sitting up in bed looking none the worse for their adventure. Sam was still on oxygen and Ruthie was having a few tears, but the nurse taking care of her said she was doing fine.

Cassie used her familiarity with the staff to ask after Mae. There was some hesitation but after a while the nurse in charge said she would try to find out.

When she came back her expression told Cassie what she couldn't say in words. Shaken she went in search of James but he had already disappeared. Assuming he had become sick of waiting for his tea and gone off to the canteen she followed him there, but when she arrived he wasn't there either.

'The four younger children can go home in the morning provided there are no complications overnight,' she was told when she returned to the ward.

'We're to stay here tonight,' cried Donald eyeing up the computer games at the bottom of the ward.

'I want to go home,' wept Ruthie.

'My chest hurts,' said Sam.

'Will Mae be all right?' asked Dorothy.

Cassie sat down between Ruthie and Sam and the twins piled on to Sam's bed. 'Mae is very poorly so we must all say our prayers

94

tonight and ask God to take care of her. Soon I have to go and tell Marc what has happened. He will want to know that you are all well and being very good until I get back. OK?'

Four heads nodded in unison.

On her way to try and contact Marc again she nearly fell over James who was back on the bench in the corridor.

'Where were you?'

'The police took me into an office over there. Did you get Marc?'

Cassie shook her head. 'I'm just on my way to try again. Come on, we'll drop off at the canteen on our way.' She told him about the children as they went and he told her about his last look at the church before he was bundled into the ambulance.

'It was well ahold, lassie. I have many doubts that it will survive.'

She left him drinking a cup of strong tea and went outside to phone.

This time it was answered. 'Say no more, Cassie, I'm on my way home. The police called me fifteen minutes ago. Is James there?'

'Yes, he's shaken but fine. I'll be waiting for you.' She switched off and made her way back to the canteen.

Cassie could not believe her eyes when she stepped out of the car and stared at the ruins of what had been the Dominics' home. The stone walls still stood but part of the roof had fallen in. Windows like empty eye sockets still

95

smouldered. All the beautiful stained glass lay in sparkling shards on the ground, crunched under the muddied chaos of firemen's leftovers.

Cassie could have wept but there was too much to do. The children were due out of hospital and it didn't need an expert to know that they had no home to return to. She would have them here, at least while Marc was to spend all his time at Mae's bedside.

Her condition was giving cause for alarm. There was talk of a leg amputation should she get well enough to withstand the operation. She had severe burns to a large area of her body and the doctors were not hopeful.

There were three spare bedrooms in the house, if she put Ruthie and Dorothy in one then Donald and Sam could have the other one and that left the other one for Marc should he need it. She made up the beds quickly, then put the heating on to counteract any leftover shock the children might be suffering, before lighting the fire in the kitchen and putting a pan of soup ready on the stove.

After staying in the hospital all night she was in need of some sleep herself but the children were expecting her back to pick them up and bring them home. James, after gaining permission from the police, had gone home to Scotland. Marc had arrived at the hospital in an incredible short time from London and after speaking to the children to assure himself that they were all well on the way to recovery had gone straight through to Mae's bedside.

He was waiting beside the children when she returned to pick them up. He stood up and taking her into his arms kissed her.

'Thank God you were here,' he said.

Four pairs of eyes, round as saucers, stared in silence before following her out to the car.

CHAPTER TWELVE

'Are you and Marc an item?' Donald wanted to know as soon as they were settled in the car.

'No, we're just good friends.'

'Everyone says that, but it's just an excuse to make things sound proper.'

'Well in this case it's the truth.'

'Is Mae going to die?' asked Ruthie.

Cassie sighed. 'We hope not, darling.'

'Can I come and live with you now?'

Cassie smiled at the little girl's persistence. 'Yes, darling, you are all coming to live with me for now.'

'Marc as well,' Donald asked, and Cassie could see trouble ahead.

'Marc is at the hospital with Mae as you very well know, Donald.'

*   *   *

Once home she showed the children their respective bedrooms then led them down to the kitchen. They were familiar with the kitchen and settled in at once. Sam played with MacBeth, Ruthie climbed into the rocking chair and began to sing to herself, while the twins plonked themselves at the table and watched expectantly as Cassie stirred the soup.

'I have a room of my own,' Dorothy voiced to no-one in particular.

'That's right she does,' Donald stated, 'Ruthie sleeps with Mae.'

Cassie dished up the soup and they were joined by the other two before Cassie said, 'Well I'm sure Dorothy won't mind looking after Ruthie while Mae is in hospital.'

'I don't mind really but she does cry sometimes.' Dorothy looked rather apprehensive so Cassie asked her, 'Does she cry at night?'

'She has nightmares,' said Donald, 'that's why she sleeps with Mae.'

Oh dear, Cassie thought. 'Then she had better sleep in my room.'

Dorothy looked relieved.

If Cassie thought she was tired before the incident of the fire she was too busy to realise just how tired she was now. The family had lost everything. They all needed new clothing from underwear to shoes and Cassie's meagre pantry could not cope with the demands of a hungry family so there was more shopping to do. Then they began to complain at lost possessions, toys, bikes, books and games.

After two hectic days, Cassie managed to get them back to school with the help of some neighbours who offered school runs. The cleaner from the village agreed to work more hours for which Cassie was grateful. Then Alf turned up one morning with two bicycles and a box of games he said his lads had grown out of.

She had called in at the hospital to check on Mae and tell the staff she wouldn't be back teaching for a while. They were very understanding and sympathetic.

One nurse that she had been rather friendly with suggested that Marc could do with some rest. 'He's looking rather worn out, it might be a good thing if you could get him to go home for a while.'

Cassie didn't like to remind the nurse that he had no home to go back to.

'He's in the canteen grabbing a cup of coffee.'

Cassie nodded and headed for the canteen. He was sitting just inside the doorway. She chewed on her lower lip as she watched him.

Unaware of her gaze he was slumped around the cup of coffee. His skin had the unshaven greyness that extreme tiredness and worry brings, he'd obviously slept in his clothes and seemed not to have eaten for some time.

Did he blame her or himself for Mae's condition? She could only guess for he hadn't said more than a handful of words to her since the fire. She'd told him she had taken the children in, and he had thanked her.

Moving forward she sat down at the table opposite him. He looked up and gave her a weary smile. 'She came round during the night, and they took her off that machine, she said a few words then lapsed back into unconsciousness again, but they seemed to think she is improving.'

'Good, I'm glad,' reaching forward she covered his hand with her own. 'I have everything ready for you at home. The children are missing you.'

He looked down at their hands on the table and sighed. 'I have to stay until she is out of danger, you know that.'

'You go home, have a little sleep, let me stay with her.'

'She might wake up again.' He spoke softly but the inference was clear.

Cassie sat back in her chair. Mae hated her and if she woke up and saw her it might do more harm than good. She nodded her acceptance of the situation and stood up. 'Is there anything I can do to help?'

'You're already helping more than I can expect taking the children in as you have.'.

*   *   *

Life settled into a strange pattern over the

next few days. Mae continued to hang on to life by a whisper but now Marc would come back to the vicarage, change his clothes, grab a couple of hours sleep and go back to the hospital again. Cassie had bought him new jeans and sweaters and made sure he had something to eat when he came back.

She and the children had rummaged through the ruins of the church and been able to claw back one or two bits and pieces.

The swimming pool roof had gone as had the conservatory, the kitchen had come off worst which was why the fire department was convinced the fire started in that area.

That the box of fireworks was to blame was not in question, what wasn't known however were the whys and wherefores that had triggered them.

The explosion had blown open the oil burning Aga and everything was covered in a thick greasy black slime. Cassie would have liked to get into the studio but the stairs and landing were so badly burnt the firemen had condemned them and taped them off.

At the front of the house, the heat that had roared through the back had blown out the windows and set fire to the beautiful carved screen that separated the entrance from the hall. The centre of the house was open to the sky and Cassie could see no way that it could ever be made back into a home again.

On the eighth day after the fire, Mae died.

The children had gone to bed and Cassie was putting a casserole in the oven for later when she heard the car in the drive. Marc was early, perhaps Mae was a little better, she thought. When she turned to find him standing in the kitchen doorway she knew it wasn't so.

She went straight to the press and fetching two glasses poured out two large brandies as he sat down heavily at the table.

'She's dead.'

Without a word she offered him a glass. Then sitting down took a sip of her own.

After a while he said, 'She was conscious at the end. Said she was sorry, but she had meant it to be your house.'

Cassie drew her breath in with a gasp, how awful for her to have carried her hatred to the grave. She watched him for any sign of blame, but he only shook his head wearily and emptied the glass.

The funeral arrangements were made and Marc sorted permission for the Chinese family to attend. The children had taken it all in their stride, only Ruthie cried for Mae in her sleep. Marc had cancelled his appearances for the next three months and James Munro was back staying at one of the guest houses in the village.

Easter was just around the corner and left Cassie wondering what on earth she was going to do with the children during the school holidays. When Marc announced that he had found a new home, Cassie felt as though she had been winded and clutched at the sink to steady herself.

'I didn't know you were looking.' She spoke without turning around.

'Come into the lounge, I want to discuss the arrangements with you.'

Slowly Cassie pulled herself up and followed him into the front room that looked more like Barbara's now than the one she had so carefully put together.

'This place isn't big enough for all of us, I'm sure you'll agree.'

She began to protest.

'Not once James is back, he can't go on living in that place forever. I'll need a studio once I start working again and the children miss the pool.'

Didn't she matter to him at all? She'd been there for them when they had needed her and now they no longer did, simple, so why did her heart ache so much?

'Where is this new place then?'

He took hold of her hands. 'I want you to come with us.'

Cassie closed her eyes and felt the warmth run through every vein in her body. The silence lengthened like rubber drawn to its furthest extreme. 'I can't, this is my home, my dream,' she whispered.

'Cassie, Cassie,' he said, drawing her closer and laying his lips on her forehead.

She pulled away and he followed her to the settee where they sat down. Staring straight ahead she said, 'I let a man into my life once before and he betrayed me in the cruellest way. I swore no-one would ever hold that power over my life again.'

She turned to face him, her glance on the long, slim fingers of his hand. 'Then you broke into my life with your children just as I was convincing myself that life was good.'

'What happened?'

She knew what he meant, and wanted to tell him, but she had never put it into words before. 'I came into a lot of money, he wanted a share, when I wouldn't give it to him he pushed me,' she hesitated, 'and I lost my baby.' There, she'd said it and it was as if someone had lifted a great burden from her. She lifted her eyes to his, she had to know his reaction.

He was smiling. Then he said, 'Come with us, Cassie, and let's make dreams of our own.'

Then she knew, this was the dream.

MS